MAGGIE MEETS HER MATCH

KYLIE GILMORE

Cover design by Sweet 'N Spicy Designs

Published by: Extra Fancy Books

ISBN-13: 978-1-942238-81-2

You rock, lady!

1

When Maggie was seventeen…before women had options

Maggie Murphy rocked back and forth on her heels, avoiding eye contact with the pack of teenaged Catholic boys gathered in the basement of St. Mary's church for the Valentine's Day dance. Her new red plaid dress with its tightly cinched belt and buttons up to her neck was as stiff as she felt. The dance floor was a wide chasm separating the boys from the girls, and no one was dancing. Father Hurley and Sister Eileen stood off to the side by a refreshment table of lukewarm punch and cookies.

She stifled a sigh. Here she was, seventeen years old, her whole life ahead of her, and all she felt was dread. Her life was already narrowly confined to two paths—go to secretary school, or, the choice her parents seemed much more enthusiastic about, marry Charles Lynch, the boy she'd known forever with bright red hair and freckles, who used to stab her with a pin in Sunday school. He worked for her parents' shoe store and they hoped he would marry her and take over the business, keeping it all in the family.

Trapped. She was trapped in the small town of Fieldridge, Connecticut, with its neat and tidy rows of ranch homes and square green front lawns. She yearned for a bigger life; her secret dream of becoming an actress seemed impossible. Respectable good Catholic girls did not up and move to New York City on their own to pursue such a scandalous career.

She stiffened. Crap. He was here. Charles shot her a quick nervous look before heading for the pack of horny teenaged boys. Charles's cowlick was especially noticeable today. He wore a V-neck navy blue sweater over a white shirt with a tie, tan slacks, and shiny brown dress shoes. He'd made an effort, and she knew she should be flattered. Maybe this was the night he'd try for a kiss. Gah. She couldn't bear the thought, and then suddenly all thoughts flew from her mind when *he* walked in. Resident bad boy Patrick "Handsy" O'Hare strode toward the refreshment table, his strong arms full of cases of soda. He'd moved into town this year, immediately making himself known as a star football player. He played a rough, aggressive game and he flippin' won games. Their school had made it all the way to State this year thanks to him.

Her friends were whispering about Patrick, everyone had a secret crush on him, but nobody dared approach him. He was a bit of a loner with a *bad* reputation. Word was he did every single thing Maggie had been warned away from—swearing, cutting class, smoking, drinking, sleeping around. He was brooding, sexy, and did what he wanted when he wanted. He lived in a trailer on the wrong side of the tracks with his mom. Some said his dad was in jail; some said he'd left them for another woman.

A flash of red hair in the corner of her eye alerted her that Charles had broken from the pack, making the trek across the dance floor to her. She practically flew to the refreshment table as if the devil himself were on her heels. Patrick was setting the soda out on the table and didn't notice her watching him. A lock of dark brown hair fell over his eyes. His hair was on the longish side, in need of a haircut to neaten it up. Like he would care! He probably said *screw haircuts, I'll wear my hair any way I please.* His shoulders were wide, his muscular arms showed off to perfection by his rolled-up shirtsleeves. He wore jeans with work boots. No jacket. The cold winter air couldn't touch this badass stud.

His lashes were thick, his cheekbones pronounced with hollows under them, his lips a little fuller on the bottom, which made her suddenly wonder what it would be like to kiss him. He kissed lots of girls, everyone knew that, the bad girls who went with him in his delivery truck or under the bleachers after a game. He'd probably be good at it.

Patrick, despite being a senior in high school, was more man than anyone she knew. Solid and strong and confident. *Say something. Anything. He's almost done unloading the soda. He's going to leave soon!*

"Handsy," she blurted, the nickname coming out much louder than she'd meant it to. It was what the school paper had dubbed him because of his extraordinary ability to catch and hold onto a football. It was also, she was sure, a reference to his skills with the ladies. She shivered deliciously at the thought.

He slowly raised sharp hazel eyes to hers. "Yeah?"

She shook her head, a strand of her light red hair catching on her rose-colored lipsticked lips. She quickly pulled her hair away from her mouth. "Hi!"

"Hey." He finished setting out the soda while she admired his large capable hands. He shifted to talk to Father Hurley, pulling a paper from his back pocket with a pen for Father Hurley to sign before turning to go.

Operating on pure instinct, an impulsiveness that had never worked in her favor, and a heady dose of lust, she followed him. "I'm Maggie."

He stopped short and gave her a full once-over, from her buttoned-up collar, lingering indecently on her boobs, waist, and the line of her hips, all the way to her beige heels. "Hi." His voice was husky, which spurred her on.

"I thought you were fantastic last season. You're a very gifted athlete."

"Thanks." He rubbed his jaw, a five o'clock shadow making him look even more manly. "That's over now. Season ended and now I gotta work."

"Is that why you cut class? To work?"

"You spying on me or something?"

"No, people talk."

He made a derisive sound and headed upstairs. It occurred to her as she admired his broad back, tight ass, and long legs that he might be able to help her out. If Handsy ruined her—as in, she was a bad girl doing terribly naughty things with the town's bad boy—Charles would drop her, her parents would wash their hands of her, and she'd finally be free to lead her ruinous life in New York City as an actress.

She rushed up the stairs behind him, and he glanced over his shoulder. "Stop following me."

"For your information, I'm heading to the ladies' room."

He stopped in the hallway upstairs and gestured toward the ladies' room.

She girded her loins. "Okay, here's the deal. There's a boy at the dance my parents have picked out for me." She lowered her voice and leaned in. "To marry." She could barely think it, let alone say it. "He's going to want to dance with me, then he's going to want to walk me home, probably think we're starting something, and it would be better all around if he had zero encouragement whatsoever."

"Don't be afraid to say no. It's easy. N-O. No."

She muttered under her breath, "Or I could go to secretary school."

Patrick heard though. "Be glad your parents can afford secretary school. At least you have a chance at a good job." His lip curled. "You with your fancy dress and shoes, whining about dancing with a boy."

"I'm trapped in this town!" she exclaimed, surprising herself. "Trapped in this life."

He lifted both palms. "We all do what we have to do to get by."

She walked right up close to him. He smelled clean like fresh soap with a hint of sexy man underneath. She went up on tiptoe and whispered in what she hoped was a seductive voice, "Ruin me."

His hazel eyes became hard, his jaw tight. "Why do you ask me to ruin you, huh? Why don't you ask me to dance with you?"

"Because you're..." *Bad.* She couldn't say that. He seemed angry. She lifted her chin. "Because you're not dressed for a dance."

He gave her a skeptical look, his lips pressed tightly together.

An old lady voice called out, "Maggie?" Crap. Sister Eileen.

"Heading to the ladies' room!" Maggie called, rushing over to wave to Sister Eileen at the bottom of the stairs. She knew the nun had a bad hip and would prefer not to make the trip upstairs.

"Okay, don't be long," Sister Eileen said sternly.

Maggie whirled, hoping desperately Patrick hadn't left. He was still here! She wasn't going to miss this chance. She grabbed his hand. "Come on," she whispered fiercely.

Luckily, he didn't pull away. "Where're we going?"

"To dance." She pulled him to the end of the long hallway by the storage closet, where they could hear the music through the vent. A little tinny, but it would do. She put her hand on his shoulder and put her other hand in his. He rested a hand lightly on her back. It wasn't awkward at all like the previous boys she'd danced with. He led them slowly in a slight sway, the space between them gradually closing until his arm was completely around her waist, and they were pressed so close the holy spirit couldn't fit. Gah! Sister Eileen had gotten in her head. *Leave room for the holy spirit when you dance!*

Patrick's voice rumbled in her ear. "You're a good dancer."

Electricity raced along her nerves, hot and tingly. "So are you."

They gazed into each other's eyes, and she leaned kissing close, barely breathing. His hand slid into her hair, cupping her head, his gaze dropping to her lips. She closed her eyes, and finally his lips met hers, gentle at first and then more firmly, his tongue spearing into her mouth, shocking her.

She broke the kiss, her eyes wide. "What was that?"

His hand slid to her jaw, his thumb stroking her cheek. "You've never been kissed before?"

She'd had two kisses, one hard, one soft, no tongue. "Not like that. Is that how you always kiss?"

His smile was slow and sure. "Yeah." He traced her bottom lip with his tongue, electrifying her, and kissed her again. This time she caught on, matching his movements and venturing to taste him too. He groaned into her mouth and pulled away.

"Where're you going?" she asked. "Kiss me and touch me and other stuff." She knew to be thoroughly ruined required more than kissing.

He stared at her mouth. "How old are you?"

People always thought she was younger than she was because she was a petite five feet one. "I'll be eighteen in April. How old are you?"

"Eighteen." He offered his hand, and she took it, hoping he'd drag her off for whatever bad boys did to bad girls, but instead he gave her hand a warm squeeze. A tingly heat rushed through her. "Bye, Maggie."

"We're not done," she informed him.

He lifted one shoulder in a careless shrug. "Meet me in the parking lot if you want."

Her heart raced. This was it! He was going to ruin her just like she'd asked. She nodded once, and he walked toward the front entrance of the church.

She dashed into the ladies' room, climbed up on the closed toilet, and opened the window up there. She knew she could make it. She'd snuck out of Sunday school more than once like this, craving her freedom. She hoisted herself up, swung her legs through, and dropped down to the ground.

She turned around and there he was, grinning at her. His smile lit up his beautiful face. He took her to his delivery truck, and things got hot and heavy in the front seat. His mouth devoured hers, and she devoured him too. The windows steamed up as his hands explored her body, not just her boobs either, his hands were everywhere, along the line of her throat, smoothing over her shoulders, down her back. She was on fire with want, straining to get closer in the confines of the cab space.

They kissed so long her lips felt bruised, her chin scraped by his stubble. His mouth trailed to her jaw and her neck, where he sucked, making her crazy. She wanted to feel him too, had never felt a man before, but just when she'd finally stroked one hand over the hard bulge straining at his jeans, he pulled away.

He stared straight ahead, his voice gravelly. "You'd better go back to the dance."

"No. I want you to do what you do to the bad girls." *Give me what I crave; give me my freedom.*

He jammed a hand in his hair, blew out a breath, and then leaned over, pushing open the passenger-side door. "Go. I have enough trouble."

And so she left on shaky legs, throbbing for a man for the very first time, aching and hot, back to the church basement. Back to her stifling reality.

2

———

Maggie had told Charles no, never going to happen, the moment she went back to the dance. Not only because she wasn't attracted to him at all, but also because Patrick had given her a taste of passion and she desperately wanted more. Charles had taken it pretty well, considering, and was dancing with another girl shortly thereafter. The real difficulty was her parents. Their disappointment weighed on her heavily, a constant tension at home.

Now it was summer, her last summer of freedom before secretary school in the fall. She hadn't been with Patrick since that one time in the parking lot, but she thought of him often. There was just something about his confidence, his complete indifference to what people thought that made her admire him. She'd seen him from a distance at school, occasionally making deliveries around town, but the few times she'd approached him, he'd given her a curt hello or a chin jerk and moved along. There was a tension in him, a strained exhausted look to his face that made her wonder what was going on in his life. Did he want out of this town as much as she did?

She tucked a stray tendril of hair that had escaped her high ponytail behind her ear as she turned onto Main Street in the early morning quiet of a sunny June day. She liked to take a long walk through town before it got too hot. St. Mary's church soon came into view. She could never think of church now without thinking of her dance with Patrick, so private and intimate, and what followed after. She heated at the memory. How could she settle for a tepid boy when Patrick had shown her the passion of a man?

She sped up past the church as if she could outrun her sexy memories. Just down the road she caught sight of workers setting up for the annual weeklong summer carnival on the large grassy field next to the firehouse. Pure joy coursed through her. The carnival was the most exciting thing to hit town. The Ferris wheel was already in place, and a crew of men were working on the Tilt-a-Whirl.

She jogged over for a closer look and slowed as her gaze caught on a tall man with rumpled caramel brown hair that curled at the nape of his neck. She lingered on wide shoulders that strained the fabric of his white T-shirt and on down to a low-slung tool belt over blue jeans with scuffed leather boots. *Manly stud alert!* She loved a man who was good with his hands.

He turned, hollered something to a short bald man with a huge neck tattoo that read Odd Todd, shook his head, and crossed directly in her path. She froze.

Patrick "Handsy" O'Hare.

Star wide receiver of Fieldridge High.

The man who had ruined her for all other boys. The man whose taste and touch invaded her dreams, made her wake hot and aching, made her yearn. The man who had barely uttered a word to her since.

His hazel eyes met hers directly. "Hi, Maggie."

"Handsy," she croaked, her throat suddenly parched. The sun had lightened his hair and bronzed his skin, making him even more gorgeous.

"Patrick," he corrected. "I don't go by Handsy anymore."

She opened her mouth to ask why, but then he was gone. His long legs ate up the distance to a white trailer with a faded star logo that read Star Carnival Productions. The metal door shut behind him.

Her curiosity and, yes, her lust had her jogging over to the trailer and knocking.

The door swung open to a scowling Patrick. "I told you I'd get it. Oh." He scanned her features, his gaze trailing over her blue and white polka-dotted summer dress, lingering on her bare legs—the dress ended mid-thigh—all the way to her feet in light blue flip-flops. He was king of the smoldering once-over. He blinked and met her eyes. "How are you?"

"I'm fine, thanks. I'm going to secretary school in the fall." At his silence, she blurted, "I took your advice and said no to Charles."

His brows scrunched together. "Who's Charles?"

She waved a hand airily. "Just the boy my parents wanted me to marry. I said no, so now they're disappointed, but it's my life, right? Anyway, what're you up to?"

A flicker of pain crossed his expression before he quickly covered with a tight smile. "Working."

She didn't know why, but she was drawn to him like a magnet. It was more than that he was the most beautiful man she'd ever slapped eyes on or that he was a fantastic kisser. She wanted to know what was going on in his life, what caused him pain. She climbed the metal step leading to the doorway where he was standing. Heat radiated off him. Or maybe that was just her, producing a furnace level of heat from standing close to him again after living with just the memory of him for so long. His jaw was deliciously scruffy with dark brown stubble she wanted to feel scraping against her as he—*focus!* "What are you doing here at the carnival? I thought you worked for the market."

He turned and went inside the trailer. She followed, slipping through the rapidly closing door, and watched him dig through a massive toolbox with lots of interesting levels and compartments. "I'm looking for a screw."

That sounded dirty and, Lord help her, she liked it. She bit back her impulse to say something dirty in return and went with the classier, "Maybe I could help." Because her mom raised her to be a lady. *Snort.*

"You don't even know what kind of screw." He waved in the general direction of the door. "It must've fallen out when we hauled in the Tilt-a-Whirl."

She couldn't help the laugh that bubbled out. "You have a screw loose?"

He narrowed his hazel eyes. "Is there something I can help you with?" Which was a nice way of saying *get the hell out.*

"Why aren't you working for the market anymore?"

He clenched his jaw. "I took a month off work to train hard for an open tryout with the New York Titans. They're a new pro football team. Didn't make the cut. Now I'm working for my uncle's traveling carnival because…never mind. This is my job for now."

It struck her that he'd at least gone for his dream. She was surprised he didn't make the team. He really was an incredible athlete. "Sorry you didn't make the team."

"Thanks," he said through gritted teeth.

This was probably the last time she'd see him before he moved on with the carnival. Something in her rebelled at that. She wanted to make him feel better, have some fun together. After all, the carnival could be very romantic. Kissing at the top of the Ferris wheel, groping in the Haunted Mansion (yes, even in summer they made good use of the old Keller House), fooling around during the fireworks at the park.

Or so she'd heard.

All of her dread about secretary school and her future, along with Patrick's current disappointment, shone a bright light on the importance of here and now. Maybe they could share the full romantic carnival experience she'd always wanted. They'd make each other feel good, even if it was temporary.

Because wasn't a week of "Handsy" fun better than nothing? Her pulse had already picked up speed just standing next to him. Imagine if he touched her again. Her mind flashed to glistening golden skin sliding against hers, drenched in desire—

"Found it!" Patrick held up a large screw in triumph. "I knew we had one in here."

She took out her hair band and shook out her long light red hair. It was probably her best feature. Not that he noticed. He was already heading for the door, brushing past her. She breathed in soap and sexy male. Her favorites.

She cleared her throat to get his attention, her brain scrambling for a classy way to ask him to have fun with her for the week, but what came out was a job suggestion. "Maybe you could coach football or…" She waited for him to fill in the blank with an appropriate verb. (Or a hilariously inappropriate one.) Obviously she'd have to work up to the more important question. "Well, what would you like to do?"

He stopped, one large capable hand on the doorknob. "What I'm going to do is fix the Tilt-a-Whirl. I'm a carnie now."

He did *not* look like a carnie. He looked like a tall, broad-shouldered, super-sexy athlete or just plain super sexy.

Fascinated, she followed him out, appreciating his tight butt as he strode to the ride that needed a screw more than she did. Probably. Lately her Patrick dreams had been extraordinary explicit. She always did have a vivid imagination. "I just don't see you as a carnie."

He turned and grinned, a move that lit up his face. All of her favorite girl parts lit up too. "Just helping out my uncle for the summer. I needed a change of scenery. We travel with the rides, setting up carnivals all over the Northeast."

"Sign me up!" Because that sounded kind of fun.

"We're all set but thanks." He winked, and before she could wink back or do anything mildly flirty, he continued on his way.

"Bye, carnie!" she hollered.

He barked out a laugh. "Bye, Maggie."

"It's Maggie Murphy. Remember that name, Patrick O'Hare."

He turned, walking backwards as he spoke. "Why? You gonna be sticking around?"

Say something flirty. "Duck!" she hollered.

His brows shot up. "Duck?" he asked right before he stumbled backwards over a duck.

She winced. A line of ducks, actually, loose from the petting zoo that was still getting set up in a corner of the field. He landed on his butt in the grass. The mommy duck squawked at him, flapping her wings before herding the younger ducks away. The tips of Patrick's ears turned red.

Something about seeing the superstar wide receiver land on his ass while getting yelled at by a duck made her heart squeeze. She crossed over to him and held out a hand to help him up.

"I've got it," he grumbled, getting to his feet.

"What are you doing later?" she asked, by which she meant *kiss me, please.*

His lips curled up in a sexy smile. Like he could hear the second version in her head. "Meet me at noon at the trailer."

He turned and walked away.

Alrighty, then. Time to get handsy. She fought the impulse to do her happy dance (in case he witnessed it) and floated back in the direction of home.

"Who's the girl, Patrick?" Uncle Todd asked, appearing at Patrick's side, where he was screwing in a reinforcement for the hinge that held an arm of the Tilt-a-Whirl together.

Patrick jerked his chin. "Just someone from school." He didn't know why he'd agreed to meet her. She was into him because of football, and football was in his past. He knew he came from nothing, that people judged him and called him trailer trash. Football had been his only hope to make something of himself. Now he had to figure out who he was without the one thing he was good at. Probably didn't help that the only girl he had real feelings for, Sandra, had dumped him for the quarterback. The last thing he needed was another girl into him for the wrong reasons. But something about Maggie Murphy and her big beaming smiles appealed to him. She didn't look at him like he was trash. She looked at him with desire in her eyes. Like he was worthy of someone like her from a good well-to-do family.

If he had a do-over, he'd focus one hundred percent on football. He'd lost focus at the state championships, upset over Sandra dumping him, distracted by her flirty attention on the sidelines for the QB. If he'd been focused, they could've won, and maybe a college would've recruited him. He didn't have the grades or the money for college otherwise. He'd never let a girl close enough to ruin his chances again. But life didn't give do-overs, so live and fucking learn.

His dark thoughts faded at Uncle Todd's grin, which showed off his gold-capped front tooth with a diamond T. His uncle was his mom's younger brother, nearly the opposite of his mom's tall, thin graceful self. Uncle Todd, or Odd Todd, as his friends and neck tattoo called him, was a short, out-of-shape nomad. There were rumors that Todd's dad was actually a magician who passed through town with a traveling carnival. Todd had run with the idea and joined the carnival that he now owned. It suited him perfectly. Patrick didn't care if the rumor was true or not, Uncle Todd was a helluva lot of fun. More importantly, football meant nothing to his uncle, who treated him just the same as always despite Patrick's failure.

"She looked like a breath of fresh bubble gum," Uncle Todd pronounced.

"Yup." He hadn't missed her bare exposed legs, the pink flush of her cheeks, her tongue darting out to wet her lips. So damn sexy. *Down, boy.* He headed to the pile of supplies a short distance away to fetch some grease for the hinges, hoping to hold off waking up the sleeping giant in his pants. He'd already had to imagine a bucket of ice down his jeans once sweet Maggie stepped close enough for him to get a big whiff of her vanilla scent. He had a real taste for vanilla.

When he returned, his uncle elbowed him in the gut. "What?" Patrick asked with a smile. This oughta be good.

His uncle took his time answering, wiping the sweat off

his face with the bottom of his white tank top. Patrick's gaze caught on the mermaid tattoo on his uncle's potbelly that he liked to make swim. It used to make Patrick crack up when he was little. His uncle dropped his shirt, met Patrick's eyes, and leveled him with a direct hit. "Wouldn't hurt you to have a little fun with someone so different from Scarlett."

"Sandra," Patrick said through gritted teeth.

Uncle Todd waved in an airy feminine gesture at odds with his short, stocky middle-aged manly self. "Now why did I think Scarlett? Oh, I know. The one time I met her, she had her nose in the air like Scarlett from *Gone with the Wind*."

"Whatever you say," Patrick mumbled. His uncle was always making some odd reference to an old movie. Truth was, Patrick had seen some of those movies with his uncle, and Sandra was a little like Scarlett—beautiful glossy sophistication with a tough-as-nails inner strength. He'd fallen head over ass in love. Never again.

His uncle started singing "All Shook Up" by Elvis. He was about as subtle as a two-hundred-fifty-pound linebacker. *Bam!* Hard tackle at the five-yard line.

"Yeah, yeah," Patrick said, getting back to work.

Patrick endured endless musical numbers from his uncle, which he knew would grate on his nerves on the upcoming long drives to the next small town in need of a carnival, but it was a small price to pay to keep his mind off football and his own uncertain future. It was hard to settle down when he'd had such big dreams. A restless energy clawed at him.

His mind drifted to Maggie. She was all sparkle and bouncy energy. Fun written all over her. If he could just keep her from bringing up football, she might be just the distraction he needed. They could hang out for the week. As friends. He didn't want to sully her and leave her, no matter how tempting she was. A lot of girls made it a game to collect as many jerseys as possible from the football team after fooling around. He'd had fun with that for a while, until he fell hard for Sandra. He'd thought they were on the same page. Turned out she was even worse than the others, looking for the best prospect to marry into big-league money.

When recruiters took an interest in their quarterback, so had Sandra.

So no more fooling around and definitely no relationships. He had to stay focused on figuring out his future without football. There had to be more for him than a trailer on the wrong side of the tracks.

3

Patrick waited on the front step of the trailer where he'd told Maggie to meet him. He planned to say right up front that any talk of football was off-limits and, if she was cool with that, they could hang out. He'd spent so much time these past couple of weeks with his carnie family—ranging from middle-aged to ancient—he was kinda looking forward to talking to someone his age.

Or not.

He stifled a groan at the sight before him. Maggie had changed into a white blouse cut low enough in front to show some cleavage, pink short pants, and flip-flops. Her curves with lots of skin showing were way more tempting than in the dress she'd had on earlier. The worst part was that she was carrying her high school yearbook. She'd probably want him to sign by the picture of him in his football uniform, and he didn't want the reminder. He pushed to his feet and met her halfway.

She came to an abrupt halt, toe-to-toe with him, and beamed. His mouth went dry. Her eyes were bright blue and sparkling with mischief. Her light red hair was long and wavy, flowing past her shoulders. He took the yearbook from her hand. *Beautiful magical goddess.*

He sucked in a breath. Where had that come from? But

goddess suited her perfectly. She was lit up from within, glowing, drawing him in.

"I thought you could sign my yearbook," she said. "Since I didn't see you at school when they came out."

"Let's skip signing stuff."

She cocked her head before saying agreeably, "Okay, if you say so."

She reached for the yearbook, her slender fingers brushing against his stomach. The touch made his brain fuzzy as all the blood drained from his head to parts further south.

She looked up at him expectantly, tucking the yearbook under one arm. Her head only came up to his chest, and her petite size made him want to spin her around for some crazy reason. She piped up. "I'm ready when you are."

Ready. Ready for what? He was about to ask, but what came out was, "I like your blouse."

She glanced down at herself. "Thanks. I made it."

He could see the outline of her bra, the sweet curve of her breasts.

"Why don't you want to sign my yearbook?" she asked.

He jerked his gaze back to her eyes. "It reminds me of football. I'm trying to put it behind me."

She bobbed her head. "Righto!"

He found himself smiling, really appreciating her not asking a bunch of questions about why he was putting football behind him. "I'll put it in the trailer." He turned and headed for the trailer. She followed, hurrying to keep up, and he slowed to keep pace with her.

"So you want to make out in here?" she asked once they were inside the trailer. "You could lift me onto the counter and we'd be nearly the same height. I'm sure you have the upper-body strength. I mean, look at you."

He glanced over, not sure if he'd heard her correctly. Did she just ask to make out? Most girls didn't speak so brashly. "What?"

"You could lift me."

"Probably."

"Cool." She set the yearbook on the far end of the counter and smiled at him.

He was smiling again for no other reason than she was so easy to be with. And beautiful. And smelled like vanilla.

Still, he'd thought they'd hang out as friends. Maggie had other ideas. She crossed to him and threw her arms around his neck.

He stood with his arms at his sides. "What're you doing?"

"What do you think?" And then she pressed her lips to his. He reacted instinctively, his hands going to her waist, kissing her back. She sucked his lower lip into her mouth, and raw lust tore through him. He took over the kiss, tunneling his fingers through her mane of hair, pressing closer, harder, sweeping his tongue inside. She tasted like cherries. That was his last coherent thought. The kiss went on and on. The next thing he knew, he had her on the counter, his hands on her ass, pressing her flush against him. Her legs wrapped around him, and then she was pulling at his T-shirt. He broke the kiss to rip off his shirt and toss it behind him.

"Ooh, Handsy," she said, running her hands over his chest. "I like this very much."

The nickname stopped him short, like a bucket of ice dumped on his head. What the hell was he doing? She was a football fan. He was probably just another jersey for her. Been there, done that many times over.

He stepped back and retrieved his shirt, pulling it back on.

"What's wrong?" she asked.

"You called me Handsy."

"Oops!"

"Yeah, oops."

"I meant Patrick. It slipped out."

He headed for the door and held it open for her. "Come on."

"So we're not getting handsy in here?"

"No."

"Patrick?"

He sighed. She was not going to make this easy. "What?"

"I really liked kissing you."

He felt himself get hard again. Didn't take much to get a rise out of him around her. "Thank you."

"Did you like kissing me?" Her blue eyes were wide and hopeful, forcing him to be honest.

"Yes."

She beamed. "Let's go on the Ferris wheel."

He was having trouble keeping up with her conversation. Of course, it didn't help that his brain was fuzzy the moment her lips met his. Before that, if he was being honest. The moment they touched.

He scratched his head, willing his brain to function again. "The Ferris wheel isn't open until tomorrow."

"Then it's a date!" She brushed past him with her sexy vanilla scent, and it took everything he had not to grab her and pull her back in his arms. Instead he followed her outside. "You want to get a bite at the diner?" she asked. "They have the best fries."

His stomach rumbled, and he welcomed the distraction from the spell he was under from this magical goddess. "Yeah, that sounds good."

They walked toward the diner just down the street.

"Sorry about the dreaded nickname," she said. "It's just we all chanted it last season. It's...you."

"Yeah, well, I can't be that guy anymore. Now I have to figure out what's next."

One corner of her mouth lifted in a crooked smile that made his dead heart stutter to life with a weird flip. "I'm in the same inner tube," she said.

His brows scrunched together. "Inner tube?"

She made a wavy gesture using her whole arm. "Floating down the river of uncertainty, trying to see what's coming up next. I mean, I know secretary school is next, but my rebel brain has other ideas. I might flee the scene. I'm not ready to be stuck in nowheresville my whole life."

He knew *exactly* what she meant. "Are you moving on to something new?"

She took his hand, her smaller one clasping his in what

felt like a gesture of support. "Just between you and me, I want to move to New York City to become an actress."

"Do you know someone there?"

"Not a soul. My parents would disown me. It's a flying leap for me. Once I jump, there's no going back."

"Maybe there's a middle ground. You could be a waitress while you audition. Maybe you could find a roommate."

She nodded. "It's the big unknown. It would definitely be easier to go to secretary school and get a job. But then I look at you and see how you went for your dream, and I think maybe I should try too."

He clenched his jaw. She might have the same terrible results as he did—failure. And then where would she be? Alone in New York City, unprotected, scraping by on tips? Maybe the best advice he could give her was just to accept that big dreams were fantasies, and she should put it behind her like he did. But the words wouldn't come out. Just thinking them made him feel like he was suffocating.

They reached the diner, and he held the door open for her. She slipped inside and held up two fingers to the hostess. The scent of grilled hamburger and fries made his mouth water.

"Patrick, I think we should go for a ride together," the magical goddess said. *Stop with the magic shit! Maggie, her name is Maggie.*

He was puzzling over what kind of ride—inner-tube thing maybe—when an old man called out, "Hey, is that Patrick O'Hare?"

He glanced over to a group of old-timers—all men—gathered in the center of the diner around four Formica-topped tables.

"It is!" one crowed. He wore a Bobcats cap. That was the high school mascot. Football was big around here. "Boy, get yourself over here. Lunch is on us. Handsy's here, everybody!"

"Handsy, Handsy, Handsy, score!" they chanted.

He held up a hand in greeting and debated how to leave without offending anyone. They'd want to talk about the state championship, and it was too painful, knowing how he'd let everyone down.

But then Maggie spoke up, rattling off their names—all eight of them—as she smiled sweetly. He caught only a few—George, Frank, Walter, Harry. "It's so good to see you all again!" she exclaimed.

The men stumbled over themselves to greet her in kind. She inclined her head, graciously accepting their gentle, "Good to see you, Maggie."

Maggie took his hand and squeezed. "He only answers to Patrick, and he's all mine for the next hour."

The men were not so easily put off.

"Aww, Maggie, we're big fans," one said. "We went to State with Handsy."

"Forget State," another said. "First game of the season he caught the game-winning pass. A miracle catch!"

"I've been giving your coach play suggestions for years," the one with the Bobcats cap said. "Frank Johnson. Has he mentioned the Long Johnson?"

Maggie giggled.

"Uh, no, sir," Patrick said. "He never mentioned the, um, Long Johnson."

Frank looked disappointed. "The Long Johnson works every time. Ya see, the secret is you've got to penetrate—"

"He said he never heard of it, Frank!" Harry barked. Or maybe it was Walter.

Frank rallied quickly, raising his arms in a V of victory before booming, "Go Bobcats!"

Patrick winced.

Maggie released his hand and walked over to the group, speaking in a low tone that he couldn't make out. She returned to him, took his hand, and led him to a booth by the window. No one called out to him again.

He sat across from her and leaned close. "What'd you tell them?"

"I told them I was working on a plan to keep you in town as football coach, and they had to let me work my magic." She gave him that crooked smile that did something weird to his heart. Her blue eyes danced with mischief, and all he could think was—yes. Yes to mischief. Yes to fun.

Yes to more kissing.

His blood heated as their gazes locked. She licked her lips. Electric energy coursed through him, making him feel more alive than he'd felt in months.

He straightened up, squaring his shoulders, deciding he might just be able to hold his head high after all. "What'd they say to that?"

"They offered to give us some of Frank's homebrew." She gestured him closer. When he leaned in, she whispered, "They say it can cause love in three days like a love potion. Of course, they were joking. It probably just leads to a lot of drunken revelry and poor decisions." She grinned.

That love part should've scared him off for good. And definitely the poor decisions. If he had any sense at all, he'd be running. Instead he was fighting the impulse to kiss her again.

"No worries, I never make poor decisions," she said, picking up the menu. "Just kidding! You don't know me well enough to know when I'm kidding, so I'll just let you know right now, I'm funny." She peeked at him over the menu. "And I make poor decisions."

He chuckled. "By homebrew you mean beer?"

She put down the menu. "I mean like moonshine. Straight-up alcohol with a chaser of fruity goodness. You can buy it at the liquor store. Hey, you want to go to a river party at Aunt Carolyn's tonight? You can bring the strawberry homebrew. Frank will help you out."

She'd taste like strawberry, cherries, and vanilla, and he'd want to eat her up. He studied her for a moment, trying to figure her out. Did she just want to hang out and have fun, or was she after a jersey? Bragging rights that she'd been with Handsy.

"You can think about it if you want," Maggie said. "But the offer of a good time expires in one hour." The corners of her mouth curled in a seductive goddess smile, reeling him in.

The waitress arrived to take their order. He glanced at the menu and quickly decided on a double cheeseburger and fries. Once they were alone again, he took a chance, asking what he really needed to know, even though it might piss Maggie off. "How many football players you been with?"

She squinted at him. "Now you're being funny, right?"

He slowly shook his head.

"You really think football player types are interested in someone like me?"

"Types?"

"Big, muscled—" her eyes dilated and his jeans got tight "—strapping jocks?"

"Yeah."

She cocked her head. "My nickname was Kooky Maggie in school."

He winced. "Ouch." That was mean.

She smiled at him warmly. "I love that 'ouch' was your reaction. Most people just laugh."

He swallowed hard. Between the warm smile and the mention of love, he'd grown unexpectedly warm all over. It must be the goddess thing. He felt enchanted. Damn, he was never this sappy. He needed his man card back.

She went on. "So, no, I didn't have football player types falling at my feet."

She should have. Those guys were idiots. Yet he found himself blurting, "So you don't collect football jerseys?"

She scrunched her nose adorably. "Why would a girl wear a football jersey?"

She wasn't a groupie.

And now he was in trouble because the very next thing out of his mouth was, "Yeah, I'll go to the party."

"Woo-hoo!" She shook her finger at him, her blue eyes dancing with mischief again. "But don't go falling for me in three days. That's just a superstition. You're not superstitious, are you?"

"Nope." Sure, he had little rituals pregame (run a lap counterclockwise around the field, slap his shoulder pads three times) and traditions to keep a winning streak going (not washing his socks). That wasn't superstitious, though. That was just smart.

She gave him a big exaggerated wink, and he wondered if she'd heard about his little rituals. Whatever. Those days were behind him. He turned and looked out the window, pushing the dark regret down.

"You want to see a salt shaker disappear?" Maggie asked.

He turned back to her, and she waved a napkin with a flourish, placing it on top of the salt shaker, then scooped up the shaker, transferred it to her other hand, and then showed him her empty palm. Classic sleight of hand.

"Very—" he started.

"Oh! What's this?" She produced the shaker from the top of her blouse, unintentionally giving him a sweet view of her cleavage. His mouth went dry.

She grinned, blue eyes dancing with merriment. "Huh? Huh?"

His desire coiled tight, his body urging him to touch and taste and devour. Damn, if he could get this wound up from a magic trick…

She handed him the salt shaker. "Ta-da!"

"Magical goddess," he muttered, reaching across the table for her hand and pulling her close for a kiss. She opened for him, her tongue darting out to touch his, and he was lost. Heart-pumping lust escalated the kiss quickly, raw and carnal, giving him a rush like he'd just crossed the end zone for the winning touchdown.

"Burger and fries!" the waitress announced, plunking down their plates with a clatter.

He jerked away from the cherry-flavored mouth he couldn't seem to get enough of. The waitress shook her head and walked away. He watched Maggie's expression. Was she mad he'd gotten carried away in a diner? Her cheeks were flushed, her eyes bright.

She picked up a fry and fed it to him. "And that was without homebrew."

4

—————

That night Patrick honked the horn right on time in the street in front of her house. She peeked out the front window and waved at him sitting in his uncle's candy-apple-red pickup truck. Sporty!

"A gentleman would come inside and meet your parents," her mom said.

Maggie bit back a smile. She sure hoped Patrick wouldn't be a gentleman tonight. Nothing like a river party to get a guy feeling frisky. "Don't worry, Mom, it's just Aunt Carolyn's. I'm sure you'll get a full report!"

"That's what I'm afraid of," her mom muttered. Aunt Carolyn was her mom's baby sister.

Maggie darted out the door. She could admit to being hepped up on hormones. She'd been rereading the dirty passages in the books she'd filched from her friend Sue's bookshelf. Sue's parents were much more open-minded than her own. She had a very good feeling that Patrick would know what to do with his large capable hands with little direction from her. Still, she figured it was better to be prepared with some book knowledge, since her actual experience so far had been a dud.

He certainly knew what to do with that mouth. She shivered, thinking of the delicious kiss he'd laid on her right at the diner table. She would've tried for more after lunch, but he had to get back to work. The carnival rides opened tomorrow, and his uncle needed him for setup. Apparently he was the youngest and strongest on the crew.

She couldn't help her smile as she reached the truck. He looked freshly showered, his caramel brown hair still damp, his square jaw clean-shaven. He wore a different outfit—button-down white shirt with jeans. Yum. "Hi, stud!"

He grinned, making her girl parts sit up and take notice. "Hey, goddess. I like your dress."

Goddess! Wow! She was a goddess? It was nice of him to notice her new cute white sundress with a red and blue pattern of bows. The best part was the exposed skin from the halter straps and full skirt that ended at the knees. She lived by the motto *Never hide your light under a bushel. Let it shine!* It was her own twist on something she'd read once. In any case, she wanted more experience, and she wanted it with gorgeous sexy Patrick. As soon as she climbed into the cab of the truck, she asked, "Why did you call me goddess? Was it the dress?"

He clamped his mouth shut and stared straight ahead.

"Patrick?"

"Uh, that slipped out. I shouldn't have—"

"O-o-o-h! That is the nicest thing anyone's ever said to me!" She threw her arms around his neck and kissed his cheek. She felt his smile in the curve of his cheek. "Did you get the strawberry homebrew?"

"Yup. It's in the back in a cooler." He put the truck in gear and pulled away from the curb.

"How do you like the carnie life?"

"I like it, but it's a temporary gig. I get paid peanuts."

"But you get a free place to live and all the kettle corn, funnel cake, and corn dogs you can eat."

"Don't forget the ice cream, cotton candy, and caramel apples."

"Exactly! All the food groups are represented—meat on a stick, dessert, and apples."

"Somehow I think you missed something."

They exchanged a grin.

He turned back to the road. "So what exactly is in homebrew?"

She grinned. "Liquid fire! You'll get used to it." She gave him directions to her aunt's house.

"Who's going to the party?" he asked.

"Everyone."

"Who's everyone?"

"I don't know. Everyone who's young enough to party will be there. Definitely my aunt, Carolyn, it's in her backyard. Probably her husband, Joe, too. They don't have any kids, which is probably why she likes to host everyone, even younger people." Aunt Carolyn, in her thirties now, had been Maggie's babysitter as a teen. Her aunt hadn't been able to have children.

"You know everyone in town?"

"Pretty much. I lived here my whole life. How about you? Where did you live before Fieldridge?"

"We lived in Queens before my mom lost her job. But we'd moved a few times before that too. Anyway, we moved here because her friend got her a waitress job at a fancy restaurant. Plus it was affordable."

"That's good."

"I guess. It must be nice to live somewhere your whole life. You know everyone, and everyone knows you."

"In some ways, yes, but in other ways…no."

"How is it bad?"

She lifted one shoulder. "Because they know you so well, they have certain expectations. Like people still think I'm a little weird because I had a pants stage freshman year."

"Pants?"

She nodded once. "I wore pants under my skirt because I thought it was very rock and roll. Dress code said girls can't wear pants, but technically I was wearing a skirt. Ever since then, I can see in their eyes people are waiting for me to do something *really* out there."

He snorted. "You? Never!"

She grinned. "When did I ever do something weird in front of you?"

"You didn't, but your mischievous eyes tell me you're plotting something."

She laughed. "I do like to have fun. Speaking of which, you and I need to have the full romantic carnival experience."

"Romantic?" he croaked.

"Yeah, you know, kiss on top of the Ferris wheel, all that good stuff."

"I really need to stop kissing you."

"Why? You said you liked it."

"I do like it, but—"

"Excellent. So I know you're a football star—"

"Don't talk about that. I'm trying to forget it."

"Oh-kay. Tell me something else about you. Something more interesting than the F-word." She giggled, feeling extremely naughty.

A slow, sexy smile dawned on his gorgeous face. "Not much more interesting than the F-word."

"So we'll just talk about that."

"Err, um, well..." he stuttered adorably.

"Just kidding! What do you like to do when you're not, you know, playing that horrible sport?"

"Nothing," he said flatly.

"You need a hobby."

"I guess."

She tapped her bottom lip, thinking. "Don't worry, I'll come up with something."

"I'm sure you will."

A short, bumpy ride later he pulled into the grassy area behind Aunt Carolyn's big old white house and parked. The backyard sloped gently down to the riverbank. Trees on the other side of the river offered some shade on hot summer days, making it perfect for lazy inner-tube rides and swimming. Tonight, though, there was a bonfire going, and people were gathered on the riverbank, hanging out. Rock 'n roll music played from a radio. Aunt Carolyn kept up with all the best music, unlike Maggie's parents.

She glanced over at Patrick, who was just sitting quietly, his expression closed off. She sensed he was sad, like maybe losing football sort of snuck up on him now and then. She fought the urge to hug him. He needed a break from dwelling on his problems, and she'd promised him a fun time tonight.

Maybe a quick kiss would help. "Patrick?"

He turned to her, and she kissed him. His response was immediate. He cupped her face with both hands, deepening the kiss, and she felt herself falling into it, into him. His lips were firm, warm, and demanding. She suddenly wished they weren't going to a party at all. He nipped her lower lip, and she moaned. His tongue swept inside, thrusting erotically, making her ache. She clutched his shirt as his hand slid up her sundress to her inner thigh, bringing a trail of electric pleasure, making her wet. She moaned against his mouth. A car horn honked, and they broke apart.

He pressed his thumb to her lower lip. "You make me forget myself."

She kissed his thumb and then held it. "Me too," she replied honestly. He was an amazing kisser, and she couldn't remember ever losing herself in a kiss like that. Like no one else existed. There was nothing but his mouth, his hands, what he made her feel, consuming her. Whoa. And that was only their third kiss.

He let out a breath. "You know I'm leaving in a week, right? The carnival's moving on."

She nodded.

"We need to stop doing that." He pulled his hand from her grip and plowed it through his hair, messing it up adorably. "I don't want to mess around or get into anything serious."

She scrunched her nose at that odd statement. "Then what do you want to do?"

"Nothing."

"Why?"

"Because I don't know what the hell I'm doing with my life, and I need to focus on that."

She squeezed his arm. "No problem! We're just having fun. Leave the homebrew here. We'll hang out on the tailgate with it after we go see everyone. Come on, they won't bite."

She hopped out of the truck, walked around to him, and took his hand, guiding him down to the riverbank, where a bunch of people were standing around talking and laughing. A sense of peace washed over her. These were her people; this was her place. She'd missed this. How could she dream of living in the city as an actress when her hometown spoke to her heart?

Her redheaded aunt spotted her just then, bubbly as ever. "Maggie! Get over here, doll!"

She grinned and made her way down the small hill to the riverbank. Aunt Carolyn swallowed her up in a big hug. "Joe!" she called to her husband. "Little Maggie's here!"

Joe headed over to say hi.

Maggie's cheeks burned. Only Aunt Carolyn could make her feel little. It wasn't like her aunt was tall either, she was just as petite as Maggie, but her aunt had been her babysitter since Maggie was three years old. Aunt Carolyn had many a story to tell about Maggie's zany antics as a kid. Was it her fault she had a big imagination and plenty of opportunity to test it out? Saddling a dog had seemed like the next best thing when she didn't get the pony she wanted. The dog hadn't agreed.

Neither had their cat.

Meanwhile, back at the river... She grabbed Patrick's hand. "This is Patrick. He's a carnie and a homebrew virgin."

Aunt Carolyn laughed. "Nice to meet you, Patrick. Go easy on the homebrew. Killer hangover material if you're not careful."

Joe showed up and gave Maggie a hug. "Good to see you." He turned to Patrick. "Hey, aren't you the wide receiver for the Bobcats?"

"No," Patrick said.

"Yeah, yeah," Joe said, pointing at Patrick. "I watched you last season. Man, you were amazing!"

"Oh yeah!" Aunt Carolyn said, seeming to recognize him for the first time. "You're the best wide receiver to come out of Connecticut since…ever!"

"Thank you," Patrick said with a pained expression.

Aunt Carolyn exchanged a puzzled look with her husband.

Maggie jumped into the awkward silence. "That was before. Now he's moving on to the next big thing."

"Oh, yeah? What's that?" Joe asked.

She turned to Patrick, who was pale and silent. Not a good way to have fun at a river party. "He's thinking about his next big move. Me too." She launched into a long monologue on the pros and cons of secretary school or following her muse at the risk of dire but artistic poverty that concluded when she ran out of air. Her aunt knew about her actress dream.

"Ooh, honey, that was a mouthful," Aunt Carolyn said. "You just take it easy tonight."

"We will!" Maggie sang. She pulled Patrick along, introducing him to everyone she knew. They spent so much time mingling, it was getting dark. That excited her because it was darkness that unleashed passion.

Her friend from high school, Donna, a copycat who used to dress like Maggie with similar unpopular results, raced over and practically tackled her in a hug.

"I haven't seen you since graduation!" Donna shrieked. She was dressed in a red blouse and orange capris. The loud colors were typical. The better to get your attention.

"That was only a week ago, Donna. This is Patrick."

Donna froze and then she asked in an astonished tone, "You're with Patrick O'Hare?"

"Yes," Maggie snapped before Patrick could deny it.

Donna spoke in a much more polite tone to Patrick. "I'm a big fan of yours. I mean your football playing."

"Thank you," Patrick said stiffly.

"Time for homebrew!" Maggie announced.

"Stop by," Donna said, gesturing to a blanket on the riverbank. "I made chocolate-chip cookies."

"Will do," Maggie said. She grabbed Patrick's hand and headed back to the truck, putting the tailgate down. "That wasn't so bad, was it?"

He leaned against the truck. "Nah."

She found the cooler in the truck bed and fetched a couple of jars for them. She handed one to Patrick and sat on the tailgate next to him. "Bottoms up," she said, taking a drink and shuddering as it burned down her throat.

He took a swig and wiped his mouth. "Blech."

"You need a little more. It tastes better the more you drink."

He took another swig and shook his head. "Boo-yah."

"Yeah?" She took a swig herself, already feeling the effects as her limbs got heavy and loose. She patted the spot next to her, and Patrick joined her.

"You got a blanket?" she asked. "We can make it like a picnic." *Or a makeout session.*

"Sure," he muttered.

He returned from the cab of the truck with a big plaid blanket and spread it out in the truck bed. He lay down, resting his head on his hands, and blew out a breath. She joined him. They stared at the dark starry sky. The moon was bright and nearly full.

"I missed this," he said. "Working the carnival, there's so many lights, it makes the stars seem dim."

"Nothing like the stars on a summer night," she said. "I'd miss this if I moved to New York City."

His head swiveled toward hers. "Are you really moving to the city?"

"That's where you go to make it big," she said on a sigh. "That or Hollywood, but I figured I'd start local, hopefully get noticed in something, and then go out west."

"That's cool."

"It's just a fantasy. I don't know if I even have a shot at making it. I might just end up moving back home, and my parents would be so mad I skipped out on secretary school, they'd say, 'Good luck, honey, you're on your own!'"

"Are you a good actress?"

Obviously Patrick had never seen her perform. And she had no idea how to answer that. How could she know if starring in her high school productions would translate to working as a professional? She sat up and fetched the homebrew, taking another swig. "Give me a strawberry kiss."

He turned on his side and propped up on one elbow. "You taste like cherries." His voice was low and husky. "I thought we agreed no more kissing."

She licked her lips, put the jar of homebrew back, and lay on her side to face him. "It's cherry lip balm, and I never agreed to that."

His large hand cupped her cheek. "Maggie."

"Patrick," she breathed.

He dropped his hand. "I don't want to hurt you." But that felt like a cop-out. Like what he really meant was *he* didn't want to get hurt.

"Why won't you do casual or serious?" she whispered. Someone must've hurt him bad. Probably Sandra Westwood, Patrick's serious girlfriend from last football season. She was the head cheerleader and had led many cheers just for Patrick. They'd broken up, though, shortly before the season ended. The gossip said she left him for the quarterback and it was why Patrick hadn't played his best at the state championship.

He rolled to his back. She took in his tight jaw and debated if she should press for details or just shut up. She impulsively ran her hand through his hair, which was so silky soft, and he closed his eyes. He needed her. She knew it instinctively. He needed comfort.

She maneuvered herself to sit behind his head, cross-legged, and tugged at his shoulders. "Rest your head in my lap." She stroked his hair again.

He shifted so her leg was his pillow, and she continued stroking his hair while he relaxed, eyes closed.

"Do you miss her?" she asked.

"Who?"

Nice try. "You know," she said, still stroking his hair. "Sandra."

"No," he said sharply. The tone meant to put her off only drew her in. He had a tender heart. Like her. She bent down and placed a soft kiss on his forehead before stroking his hair again. His expression relaxed.

She gazed at the sky for a moment. "Sometimes you have to grab life with both hands, and sometimes you just have to let go. Me, I like to let go and see what happens. Usually, it's something good." She looked down at him; he was stargazing too. She stroked his hair, loving the feel of the silky strands.

He snorted. "Not much good has happened in a while."

"How about, just for this week, you be like me and let everything go? Just have fun."

He looked up at her. Even with the upside-down view, he was sexy, all square jawed, his lips smooth and sensuous. "What does that mean?"

She stroked his jaw, reveling in the smooth hard line. "It means if I want to kiss you, you let me, and know that I like it as much as you. If I want to touch you, please, by all that is holy, let me. You're as beautiful as Michelangelo's *David*. That's a statue."

His lips played at a smile. "I know it's a statue."

"I won't hurt you, and you won't hurt me. Okay?"

He groaned. "Maggie."

She gave him her best seductive smile. "We need more homebrew." She pushed his shoulders, and he sat up. She crawled over to the tailgate and snagged the jar. She offered it to him and he took it, his eyes hot on hers. "Do it, do it," she chanted.

"How can I hold out against that?" He took a swig, and she cheered. He grinned and handed it back to her. They did a few rounds like that, swig and grin, swig and grin, before it turned to swig and hot look.

She took a last sip, set the nearly empty jar out of the way, and scooted back to his side. Their gazes locked for an electric moment before they slammed together, their mouths fusing in a frenzied kiss, their hands grabbing everywhere. Someone moaned. Her. They fell to the blanket in a tangle of arms and legs. She wanted to feel all of him, all at once, and then he was on top of her, his hardness pressing against her softness. His mouth shifted to her jawline and over to her ear. He tugged her earlobe between his teeth. "Let's go somewhere private," he whispered.

She opened her mouth to make a suggestion of where they could go, but lost her train of thought as he rained hot open-mouthed kisses down the side of her neck. She ran her fingers through the soft hair that curled at the nape of his neck.

He lifted his head and looked at her. "Are your parents home?"

She cringed. "Yes. What about your trailer?"

"I share it with my uncle."

She groaned. They slammed together again. He cupped her breast, strumming over the hard tip, making her throb. This was crazy. There had to be somewhere they could go. She tried to think, but then his mouth replaced his hand, suckling her breast through the fabric, and every rational thought flew from her head. His hand slid down her body, snagged the edge of her dress, and then slid up her inner thigh. She let her leg fall to the side, open and aching for him.

The sound of voices reached them, one of them her aunt, who would never let her live this down. She still saw her as little Maggie, the niece she used to babysit. She shoved Patrick's shoulders. He lifted his head, his lips wet from where they'd been suckling her. His eyes were dark and hot on hers. "What?"

"Get up! My aunt's almost here."

He scrambled off her.

By the time Aunt Carolyn stopped next to the tailgate and invited them down for s'mores, they were both under control. More or less.

~

It might've been the homebrew talking, but Patrick felt happy for the first time since he'd had to say goodbye to football.

Maggie made him feel light. Okay, he was drunk. He must be, because everything she did or said felt magical. His magical goddess brought him back to life. Her voice was a happy song, her beautiful smile a sunshiny day, and her body a decadent dessert. Even drunk, he knew a good thing when it landed in his lap.

As Maggie was now. They were in his truck parked at the end of a long gravel driveway of someone's horse farm, way out in the middle of nowhere. The trees lining both sides of the driveway gave them privacy. The house was dark.

She straddled him, kissing and nipping along the side of his neck.

He breathed in vanilla, cherries, and strawberries, and tightened his hold on her hips, fighting his instinct to plunge deep inside her body. He wanted her something fierce. More than he'd ever wanted anyone. And he'd had lots of football groupies throwing themselves at him. "Maggie," he managed.

She lifted her head. "Call me goddess," she whispered. "I really like that."

He groaned. She wanted his nickname for her. He loved that. It made her feel like his. She got more irresistible by the minute, and he got surprisingly possessive. He never cared enough to get possessive. Not since his ex. "Goddess, we should stop."

She frowned. "I'm having fun."

He leaned his head back on the seat. He was about to bust the zipper on these jeans. Things were getting dire with this woody.

And then she got off his lap and unzipped him.

The relief of just cotton briefs was stunningly good. She gathered her long light red hair and held it up to him. "Hold this," she said.

He knew where she was going with this, but he wanted to bring her pleasure first. He tangled her hair in his fist, pulled her in, and gave her a hard kiss. She kissed him back passionately, making these little noises in the back of her throat that had him pulling her back onto his lap and bunching up her dress. He slipped his hand under the side of her panties and slid a finger inside her. She clenched around his finger and threw her head back.

"Wait," she gasped. "I want to—"

"You first, goddess." He stroked her, slow circles, rapid flicking, everything aimed at her pleasure. She clung to his shoulders in a tight grip. He used his other hand to pull down her dress and brought her nipple to the roof of his mouth, suckling hard as he increased the pressure over her sweet spot, strumming and circling and thrusting, soaking his fingers with her desire, his own desire coiling tight right along with her. She tensed against him, and he kept going, watching her as her eyes fluttered closed, her lips parting as tiny gasps escaped. She trembled in his arms, and then she cried out, rocking mindlessly against his hand. His cock got thicker, harder, but he didn't push for more, just let her ride it out.

She sagged against him, and he slid his hand away, holding her by the hips. He felt content just to hold her, which was weird considering how turned-on he was. Her petite size fit against him perfectly. She felt right.

She hugged him. "I knew you'd be good with your hands."

A laugh rumbled out despite his dire blue-ball state. He couldn't remember ever smiling or laughing as much as he did when he was with her. His goddess.

She lifted her head and beamed. His heart stuttered.

She slid off his lap, went to her knees, and licked her lips. "Your turn."

And then she proceeded to show him the ecstasy a determined goddess could give to a guy. Her hair fell in soft waves over his lap, her mouth hot and wet, the suction hesitant at first, and then fucking perfect. He wasn't going to last long. He closed his eyes because her bobbing head was making him want to thrust hard. He panted, trying not to—

"Maggie," he warned, tugging her hair.

She moaned and took him deeper. He couldn't hold back. He exploded with a roar, jerking uncontrollably as she took in every last drop. She swallowed and licked him clean. He'd never seen anything sexier. He couldn't speak, he had nothing to say anyway; he was in a stupidly stunned state of wonder.

She lifted her head and kissed him tenderly.

He was a goner.

5

———————

Patrick's voice came out hoarse. "This might be the blow job talking—"

Maggie laughed, a joyful bubbly sound that had him grinning. "Your blow job talks?" She propped a hand under her chin. "Fascinating!"

Patrick laughed as he buttoned and zipped his jeans. He couldn't believe he was going to do this. He never mixed friends and his carnie family because, well, his carnie family was a little different—unique, to say the least—and he couldn't bear it if his friends judged them. But Maggie was different, a little unique herself, and he wanted to keep her around. He knew his offer would naturally lead to her meeting everyone.

He offered anyway. "You want to help out with the carnival? You could take pictures for some new flyers. My uncle couldn't pay much, or anything." He'd seen Maggie taking pictures around school before.

"I'd love that! I was yearbook photographer, and I have my own camera and darkroom. Pictures would really sell the event. My mom could make copies at her work."

"Sure, that would be great. Take pictures of the rides and games while we're in town."

"Can I take pictures of the carnies?"

He knew she'd want to meet everyone. Still, pictures of the carnies?

"What?" she asked.

"You'll have to ask my uncle. I should warn you the carnies are kind of different."

"Different how?"

"I don't know. Just unique."

"Like me?"

"Like…" He didn't know how to explain. Much more unique than her, and she was plenty unique. He'd known his uncle's second family his whole life and never thought anything was odd or different until his friend met them for the first time in fifth grade. The word *freak* had been uttered one too many times for Patrick's liking. He'd given his friend a bloody nose and hadn't introduced any friends to his carnie family since then. "Never mind. You'll see."

"I can't wait! Too bad it's dark. I'd like to get started right away."

"Now? Aren't you tired?"

She wiggled in her seat. "I'm full of energy. Orgasms do that for me." She blushed and looked away. "That was my first with a man, though."

He choked on a laugh. Most girls didn't speak so freely. He really liked that about her. "I feel like I could sleep right now."

She stroked his hair, relaxing him even more. "Well, you've been doing physical labor all day."

"I've done more in training. Bah. Never mind. Old news."

She gave him a quick kiss. "Now you're in a different kind of training. For the next part of your life."

He smiled. "I like that."

She kissed him gently. "I like *you*, Patrick."

His heart did that weird flip again. He loved hearing his real name from her lips instead of a football nickname that brought with it expectations and disappointment. "I like you too."

She beamed, and he just soaked her in for a moment

before starting the truck and pulling back out onto the main road.

They were halfway to her house when she informed him matter-of-factly, "You need to buy condoms tomorrow. It's easier if you do it; otherwise one of my many relatives will see me and tell my parents."

Her frankness no longer surprised him. The truth was, he wanted her. Clearly she wanted him. But some part of him worried about fooling around with someone and then leaving town. Of course, they'd already orgasmed together. Hmm...

He glanced over at her, and a bone-deep honesty and sense of fairness had him blurting, "You do know I'm heading to the next town in a week, right? Monday morning we pack up, and we might never see each other again."

"Or we might," she sang.

"I really don't want to hurt you."

"Which is exactly why you won't. I love that about you."

A rush of warmth filled his chest, almost like pride and something altogether tender. Her faith in him touched him deeply.

She went on happily. "Besides, you promised me the full romantic carnival experience, and I'm collecting on that promise."

"Exactly what does that mean?"

She lifted a finger. "Kiss on the Ferris wheel."

"Uh-huh. We covered that."

She held up two fingers. "Groping in a dark corner of the Haunted Mansion."

"Yeah?"

"Oh yeah. It's *expected*."

Odd, but okay. "Sure, I'll grope you."

She laughed. "Excellent. And last, but certainly not least, fooling around during the fireworks."

"Outside?"

"Yup."

"Next to everyone else who's fooling around?" Because, while he was open-minded, that was just a little too out there even for him.

"We'll find a private spot. You in?"

"Hell yeah."

"You please me, Patrick," she said in her funny adorable way. And all he could think was he wanted to spend the rest of his life pleasing her.

He shut his mouth so he wouldn't spout any of that weird forever shit. It was way too soon. They'd be going their separate ways in a week. It must be the blow job talking. Geez. Shut up, blow job.

Patrick had just finished helping set up the food stands—the rides were all ready to go for opening at five o'clock tonight—when he saw Maggie heading his way. She wore a light blue halter top with a matching blue and white polka dot skirt and her flip-flops. So damn cute. She gave him a big wave with a sunny smile. He raised a hand, soaking her in as she approached. Her long light red hair was up in a high pony-tail, bouncing along in time with her bouncy stride, and he wanted nothing more than to pull the hair band out and run his fingers through all that glorious hair.

She stopped in front of him, her blue eyes sparkling with mischief or fun. Either way he loved that look in her eyes. "Hi!" she said sunnily.

He cleared his throat, which was clogged with too much feeling too soon. "Hi."

She bounced on the balls of her feet. "So when do I get to meet Odd Todd? I saw his neck tattoo. Do you have any tattoos?"

He focused on the last question. "No."

"I want one."

He suppressed his shock. *Scandalous for a woman.* It seemed Maggie was a bit of a rebel. He liked that *a lot.* "Where?"

She pointed to her ankle. His gaze riveted on the spot, the long expanse of smooth bare leg. He wanted to lick it. Just the thought had his cock perking up. Ice-cold water, he thought furiously, hoping to hold off an embarrassing woody. He wore shorts today, mostly because the jeans had been uncomfortably tight around her, but a tent in his shorts would be hard to hide. He was pretty much screwed no matter what he wore as long as his magical goddess was around. *Not mine*, he reminded himself.

"You didn't ask me what kind of tattoo," she said.

"What kind?"

"A goddess. Maybe Aphrodite, what do you think?"

Wasn't that the goddess of love? Hey, he knew stuff. Did that mean…? He jerked his gaze from her smooth ankle back to her eyes. "Because of me?"

She bit her lip, smiling and nodding.

He wanted to say, *Are you crazy? Don't mark your body permanently for a guy you barely know!* But another part of him —a newly possessive side—liked it. She'd be marked with his claim. His nickname for her. A surge of lust ran through him, and he snagged her by the hips, pulling her close. He spoke near her ear. "I want to lick your leg from your ankle all the way to the top."

"You can," she whispered back.

"And a lot of other places," he added, wrapping his arms around her waist to pull her flush against him. He knew she could feel how much he wanted her, and he didn't care. "I need to get you someplace private. I got the condoms." He'd stolen them from his uncle's sock drawer.

"Patrick," she breathed. His real name on her lips turned him on so much. Hardly anyone around here, not even his ex-girlfriend Sandra, called him Patrick. Hell, everything she did got him going.

He brushed his lips over hers. "Maggie."

"So we finally meet!" his uncle's voice boomed. Maggie startled, and Patrick reluctantly pulled away. He quickly adjusted himself. Not that his uncle noticed, his sharp gaze was on Maggie.

Patrick found himself holding his breath. His uncle always said he could tell everything he needed to know about a person the first time he looked in their eyes. He wanted his uncle to pronounce her good people, to see what Patrick saw.

"Aren't you a doll?" Uncle Todd asked. He turned to Patrick and mouthed, "Good people," which filled Patrick with equal parts pride and relief. Of anyone in his family, he valued his uncle's opinion the most because he was the best person Patrick knew.

"It's so nice to meet you," Maggie said, offering her hand to his uncle. "I'm Maggie."

Uncle Todd gave her a hearty handshake. "And I'm Patrick's uncle, Todd, but my friends call me Odd Todd. I have no idea why." He turned and pointed to the tattoo on the back of his neck.

Maggie laughed. Then she looked from his uncle to him. "You don't look alike. I never would've guessed you were related."

"Poor Patricky took after his mom instead of his uncle. Damn unlucky in the gene pool."

Maggie beamed, her eyes sparkling. She took Patrick's hand and squeezed. "I'll say."

"Patricky—"

"Patrick," he corrected his uncle. Talk about a cock block. Patricky was his nickname as a kid, and only his uncle called him that anymore. Seriously, he wanted his goddess to see him as a sex god. And *Patricky* was not a sex god.

"Sorry," his uncle said. "Patrick, or should I call you Mr. O'Hare?" He raised his brows in a comically wide-eyed impression of innocence.

"That would be acceptable," Patrick replied with a straight face.

Maggie was biting back a smile, which just egged them on.

Uncle Todd made a sweeping bow. "Yes, of course, Mr. O'Hare. With your permission, I'd like to speak to the lovely lady about our flyers."

Patrick lifted a hand and made a royal rolling gesture. "You may do so."

"Thank you," his uncle said. "Ever so kind. Miss Maggie…what's your last name?"

Patrick lost his smile. He couldn't remember her last name. Talk about moving fast. *Got the condoms! Let's screw for the rest of our lives! Who are you again?*

"Miss Maggie Murphy," Maggie replied with a smile. "If you don't mind, I'd love to take pictures of the carnival and the people who work here too."

"I'm okay with that," his uncle replied. "In fact, I'd love it. Let me just check in with everyone else and make sure the picture-taking thing is okay. Some of my staff likes to lie low, so to speak, and they might want to keep it that way."

By lie low, his uncle meant they had no ties except to the carnival. They were ghosts and liked it that way.

"No problem," Maggie said. "I completely understand. I'll wait to hear from you before I start taking pictures."

"That won't be necessary," his uncle said. "I trust Patrick's judgment."

Patrick felt a twinge of guilt. It wasn't like he knew her all that well. He just wanted to spend as much time as possible with her before their time ran out.

"I'm afraid I don't have a big advertising budget," his uncle said. "So, what do you think about—"

"No payment necessary," Maggie interrupted.

"I have to pay you something," his uncle said.

"It's no trouble at all," Maggie said. "You can pay me in unlimited carnival rides and food."

"Good deal," his uncle said, and they shook on it.

Maggie turned to him and grinned. "Patricky owes me a Ferris wheel ride."

And just like that, he was turned on again. He didn't even care that she was teasing with his kid nickname, he remembered the three steps to a romantic carnival—kiss, grope, fool around—and he was eager to get started.

He grabbed her hand, entwining his fingers with hers. "Tonight," he told her. "When I'm on break after my shift on the Tilt-a-Whirl."

"Then I know what I'll be riding," she said with a mischievous grin. And she probably meant the Tilt-a-Whirl, but his body got a very different message.

Uncle Todd cleared his throat. "Come on, I'll introduce you to everyone. It'll help them decide on the picture thing if they meet you."

"Let's go," Maggie said.

"We still have some games and food to set up, so I'll just call a quick staff meeting." His uncle pulled a walkie-talkie from the belt loop on his jeans and pressed the button on the side. "Papa Bird calling. New egg in the nest. Roosting at the carousel at now o'clock."

Maggie grinned. "I've never been an egg before."

Patrick bit back every weird sexual egg joke that immediately came to mind. *Bend over easy? I'd love to crack you open and suck out all your…yolk. Maybe not.*

They came from all over the field, some from the surrounding trailers, some from the kitchens of the food stands, some from the wooden stands for games still being set up. He took in each familiar face, pure affection for his second family spreading through him. He glanced at Maggie to see her response.

"I wish I had my camera," she murmured.

He stiffened, worried she saw only oddities, but then she turned to him and smiled. "I just know there's a story here that brought this collection of people together."

There was. Every single person had a strange journey that brought them to the carnival, where they stayed, making a family of their own together.

He relaxed, wrapped an arm around her, and kissed her hair. "They're going to love you." He was already halfway there himself.

Oh, shit. He couldn't fall for Maggie. He had nothing to offer her. What was he going to do, ask her to move into the trailer with his mom? Join him on the road, working for peanuts?

He dropped his arm, but he couldn't take his eyes off her as she took in his carnie family for the first time.

6

The first thing Maggie thought upon meeting the carnies was —these are my kind of people. The second thing she thought was she had to capture their story through pictures. And then she wanted to sit over lemonade and funnel cake and *hear* their stories. She approached a tall thin man with wispy gray hair wearing a plaid button-down shirt paired with a clashing plaid kilt and old red flip-flops. His knobby knees were bare.

"Let me guess," she said, "Scottish?"

"No." The man turned to Odd Todd. "Why do people always ask me that?"

Todd shrugged, and when the man turned back to her, Todd rolled his eyes behind his back.

She grinned. "No reason at all. I'm Maggie, and you are…"

The man inclined his head. "Sir Kenneth, at your service."

"Just because I tapped you with my sword doesn't mean you're a knight," a middle-aged woman with short marsh-mallow-Peep-yellow hair huffed, appearing at Kenneth's other side. "I'm Sally, also known as the knight in shining armor when a costume is called for. Funnel cake operator when it's not." She bared her teeth in what passed for a smile.

"I love funnel cake!" Maggie said. "And knights."

"Then we'll get along just fine, young Maggie," Sally

pronounced. She reached out her right hand to shake, and that was when Maggie realized her arm was deformed. Only two small stumps protruded where a hand would've been. Maggie shook her stumps instead.

Sally smiled for real then.

Patrick took Maggie's hand and squeezed before continuing with the introductions. There were thirteen of them, including Todd. She was surprised to meet four elderly brothers, the Fellinis, in their eighties. Maybe even nineties. They moved slowly. Two used walkers; the other two leaned heavily on canes. She had to wonder how much work they could do with setup and then running a carnival. She made a mental note to ask Patrick about them later. She stopped short at an older woman wearing a darling vintage periwinkle blue dress with sheer three-quarter sleeves and a layered gauze skirt. Probably from the 1920s.

"I love your vintage!" Maggie exclaimed.

"Ha! I knew it'd come back in style. I never stopped wearing it!" Her face and neck were marked with discolored skin, maybe from an old burn. She preened and did a little runway walk. "Now they all want my duds."

"No one wants your ratty old clothes, Mallory," Sally said.

"Says you!" Mallory snapped. She turned to Maggie. "You should check out my closet. Maybe you'd like to buy something?"

"I'd love to!" Maggie exclaimed.

"No money is changing hands," Odd Todd said. Mallory's face fell. "I called you all here for a quick heads-up. Patrick's lady here is working on flyers for us."

Maggie glanced up at Patrick to see if he minded his uncle calling her his lady. He smiled at her with such warmth in his eyes, she couldn't help but melt.

Odd Todd went on. "She'd like to take pictures of us all and pick the best shots for the flyers. If you'd like her *not* to take your picture, you can let me know in private later."

"I don't mind!" a rich baritone voice called.

Maggie turned, her jaw dropping at the vision and sounds of—she blinked—yes, he really was…an accordion-playing cowboy. He wore a ten-gallon hat, fringed vest over a plaid button-down shirt, leather chaps over denim, and cowboy boots. Everything was perfect except why an accordion? His hair was black, flowing to his shoulders, his skin was bronzed. Quite stunning.

He stopped directly in front of her and tipped up the brim of his hat. "Howdy. I'm—" he paused dramatically "—the Jazz Polka Cowboy."

"Oh!" she exclaimed. "Wait, what's jazz polka?"

He smiled, his white teeth brilliant against his bronzed skin. "It's what I play, heavy jazz with a drop of polka, care of the accordion."

"That is so cool," she breathed.

He squeezed the accordion in and out in a long harmonic sound of agreement. "It's not appreciated like it should be, but I hope the people will catch on."

"Have you ever tried guitar?" she couldn't help but ask. "That might be more popular combined with the cowboy outfit."

"Pfft. I will wait for my preferred style to catch fire."

"Wish it would," Sally muttered.

"He can't play guitar," Odd Todd chimed in.

"That too," Jazz Polka Cowboy replied.

Her fingers itched for her camera. This had to go on the flyer.

Odd Todd clapped. "Okay, you've met the new egg. Let's get back to work. Curtain call is four for a live show at five!"

Everyone hustled back to their stations, except the four elderly brothers, who took forever to cross the field, headed in the direction of a large trailer.

"Well?" Patrick asked.

Her mind was spinning with ideas. It was like a theatrical show—the townspeople were the audience, and the carnie people were the actors. Each with a story to tell. Each story combining to make something new in a crescendo of colors and textures and joyful chaos.

She turned to him. "I hope everyone will be okay with pictures. This might be the best project I've ever done!"

He looked away, his jaw tight.

"What's wrong?" she asked.

He met her eyes briefly; his were suspiciously shiny. He rubbed one eye with a fist. "I'm fine. Something caught in my eye." He kissed her cheek. "I'll see you tonight."

She watched him head over to his uncle to help with the mechanics of a ride while she puzzled over what in the world would bring a tear to his eye.

~

Patrick worked the Tilt-a-Whirl that night, a now familiar sense of celebration coming over him at the sights and sounds of opening night of the carnival. It probably helped that his uncle psyched everyone up with the few days of "rehearsals" before "the show." His job was easy—take the tickets, make sure the kids were tall enough to ride, and then press the buttons to slowly start and then stop the ride. He'd work several rides in rotation, but he was most looking forward to his break when he could ride the Ferris wheel with Maggie.

She was amazing.

And she had a hold of his heart.

When he'd seen her complete acceptance of the people he loved like a second family, that not everyone could appreciate, it got him choked up. He'd had to hide an annoying tear that stung his eye.

He sensed the moment she got in line for his ride, meeting her eyes where she stood behind a group of teenaged girls. She wiggled her fingers and gifted him with a beaming smile. His heart kicked up. Just the sight of her could do that to him.

"Hey," he called. "Gimme ten minutes for my break."

"I want to go on your ride first."

He nodded once and turned back to the ride. When it finished, he waited for the riders to exit before opening the gate and watching the new group of riders go through, counting heads and making sure they were tall enough.

"Your uncle gave me the all clear for pictures," she said as she went past.

"That's great," he called.

A few minutes later, after checking all the safety bars were latched, he started the ride. He found himself watching every time Maggie whipped past. Her long hair was down and blowing crazily in the breeze, flying all over the place. She looked like she was having a blast, at first. By the middle, she looked worried and then kinda sick. When she got off the ride, she was green.

He locked the ride, locked the entrance gate, and rushed over to the exit to check on her. "Are you sick?"

"Just a little dizzy," she said, and then her eyes rolled up in her head and she collapsed at his feet.

Oh shit. He pulled out his walkie-talkie and called for his uncle before kneeling at her side. He pushed her hair out of her face. "Maggie, wake up. Come on, goddess."

Her eyes fluttered open, and she moaned, turning on her side toward him. Her hair, in crazy disarray from the ride, fell in her face. He gathered the mane of hair and pulled it back from her face. "Are you okay?"

She moaned. "Your uncle paid me too much."

"What?"

"Too much funnel cake and corn dogs," she managed before puking. He jerked back just in time, still holding her hair.

Aww, man. This was not his forte, dealing with sick.

She wiped her mouth with the back of her hand. "Sorry."

"It's okay."

He tried not to look at it. He should get back to work. Yet something kept him by her side, holding her hair back from her face just in case—

She puked again.

"I don't think you should do the Ferris wheel tonight," he said when she was done. When it looked like she wasn't going to be sick again, he released her hair and pushed it back over her shoulders.

She sat up and frowned. "You're probably right. I need to get home." She sniffled. Uh-oh. This was not his forte either, dealing with female tears. "I was so looking forward to tonight. We've only got seven nights to be romantic."

Romantic wasn't his forte either, but he had a feeling she meant more orgasm romantic than grand-gesture romantic, which he definitely could do. His uncle arrived, looked down at Maggie, and then turned to him in silent question.

"She's sick from too much carnival food," Patrick explained.

His uncle nodded. "I got the ride. Go ahead and take her home."

"Thanks," Patrick said. He pulled Maggie up, and she wobbled on her feet. Her lower lip trembled. What he did next came naturally—scooped her up and carried her cradled in his arms back to his trailer. He'd let her rest a bit before a ride in the truck. She trembled in his arms, leaned her head on his chest, and let out a shuddery sigh. It was the craziest thing. He should be completely turned off by what he'd just witnessed, but all he wanted to do was hold her hair back until she was done with the sick and then hold her trembling body until it stilled in peaceful sleep.

He set her back on her feet when he got to the trailer, one arm around her waist as he opened the door. He guided her in and puzzled over his next move. His bed was the sofa. It pulled out, but he couldn't set it up without letting go of her.

"Do you think you'll get sick again?" he asked.

"I don't think so. I just need to rest a little, and then I'll walk home. It's not too far."

"You sure?" he asked, but she was already settling on the sofa, curling onto her side. He hurried to fetch a trash can and placed it nearby. Then he got his blanket from the top of the small closet and covered her with it. There wasn't room for both of them. He'd end up pushing her right onto the floor if he tried to squeeze in there.

He sat next to her on the floor and held her hand. A moment later, she was asleep. He listened to her breathe while he silently freaked out. Because if he wasn't turned off by sick, there wasn't much else she could do to shake him loose. But they only had this week, and he had absolutely nothing to offer her.

If only he'd met her when he was at the top of his game with a chance at a bright future instead of now when he had nothing. But he couldn't turn away the chance to be with her even if it was just for a week. She was the best thing that had happened to him since he left football.

He shook his head at the wonder of it all. He honestly never thought he could feel this good without a football in his hands.

7

Maggie woke the next morning in her own bed, feeling so-o-o much better. She'd gotten a little crazy with the carnival food. Not just funnel cake but also French fries, lemonade, kettle corn, and way too many corn dogs. That couldn't be helped. The guy who worked the corn dog stand, Quinn, sang when he took orders *and* when he counted change. In fact, he never spoke once. His voice was deep and melodic, and she loved it. He was early thirties with striking good looks—black hair, blue eyes, tall, and ropey with muscles—that made him incredibly photogenic. She hung around, getting in line over and over again to listen to him and snap pictures. Over a short break, Quinn sang his story to her. He'd been mute for years due to a terrible stutter. It was Odd Todd who'd discovered the reason and gotten him singing on their long drives. He'd discovered he didn't stutter when he sang. It was all so amazing. She'd never known singing could do that.

She took a shower and brushed her teeth, remembering how sweet Patrick had been, carrying her to his trailer in the biggest swooniest romantic gesture she'd ever experienced. She was, of course, mortified that she'd tossed her cookies in front of Patrick on the night they were supposed to be kissing on top of the Ferris wheel, but he'd been really cool about it.

After a short nap in his trailer, she'd thanked him and walked home.

Today was a fresh gorgeous summer day, and she couldn't wait to get to work on her new project. She saw it more as a beautiful photographic collage than a flyer, and she knew she'd have way too much material to work with the way her ideas were flowing, but she didn't care. She hadn't felt this jazzed about a project ever. This morning, the staff was on cleanup duty, and she wanted to capture some of that action too. By noon, everything would open again. Patrick would be working some of the game booths in rotation—ball and bucket toss, milk bottles, dart balloons, and a basketball hoop game.

When she arrived at the carnival grounds, she didn't see Patrick. She decided to be stealthy and snap pictures without interacting with anyone just to capture the staff's natural demeanors. The Fellini brothers with canes were using long-handled sticks with points on the end to pick up litter, tossing it into garbage bags hooked on the front of their two brothers' walkers. It was a tandem, slow dance of cleanup but beautiful in its way. One of them caught her taking pictures and winked. She wiggled her fingers at him but kept her distance so they'd keep working. She'd even dressed in her least flashy plain light blue shirtwaist dress so she'd blend into the background.

"What do you think you're doing?" a female voice full of authority demanded.

She whirled and came face-to-face with Alice Taylor, one of Aunt Carolyn's friends, who was definitely not wearing the typical Fieldridge summer wear. Alice's silk blouse, pencil skirt, heels and leather handbag screamed rich. Though it was early morning, Alice looked sharp. Intelligence glared from her icy blue eyes, her blond hair was long and perfectly styled, her skin flawless and perfectly made up. All of that combined with the authoritative voice made her a little intimidating. Okay, a lot. Maggie couldn't seem to find her voice.

"I said what are you doing?" Alice pressed. "Why are you

taking pictures of litter and the carnival in disarray? Are you with the press?"

Maggie finally found her voice. "Not at all! I'm Maggie Murphy, Carolyn Davie's niece."

Alice studied her for a moment. "Oh, that's right. I saw you at the river party with Handsy."

Maggie nodded. "The carnival company hired me to take pictures for their flyer. I was the high school yearbook photographer." Though working for corn dogs wasn't exactly *hired*. More like volunteer work. She kept that part to herself.

Alice stared at Maggie's camera. "So you're putting pictures of litter on their flyer?"

Maggie shook her head. "No, not litter. I'm taking pictures of the people that work behind the scenes, bringing a personal touch to the carnival company."

"I'd like to see the pictures."

"I'd be happy to share. The men cleaning up are brothers, I also got Quinn the singing corn dog guy singing to a little girl who's all smiles, holding her dad's hand. Really special moments like that."

"It's connection," Alice said. "That's what you've captured. I work for the mayor. Stop by the diner tonight at five. We'll talk over dinner about you taking some pictures for the town." Alice turned on her heel and continued across the field, her keen eyes taking stock of the carnival as she moved.

Maggie let out a breath and got back to work. The carnival rides and booths without carnival goers had an almost eerie ghost town feel. All the bright multicolored lights were dark, the rides still and quiet, the game prizes covered with tarps. It wasn't something that would work on the flyer, but she found herself taking pictures anyway. It spoke to her theatrical soul —all the untapped potential of rides and games and food just waiting to roar to life with the people who would soon enjoy them. She loved contrasts like that.

"Hey, goddess," a now familiar voice called.

She turned and her heart squeezed as she took in Patrick heading right for her with a smile that lit up his face. He was the definition of male beauty from his rumpled caramel brown hair to his square jaw to broad muscular shoulders and biceps stretching a white T-shirt. But it was more than that. He held her hair back when she was sick. He carried her cradled in his arms. He worried about hurting her feelings. He *cared*.

So did she. A lot.

She tucked her camera in her purse, set it down, and ran to him, wrapping her arms around him in a big hug.

He laughed, giving her a squeeze. "I see you're feeling better."

She gave him a smacking kiss on the mouth. "Thank you for last night. I know I was no fun."

"No problem." He nuzzled into her neck and then whispered in her ear, "You up to the Ferris wheel tonight?"

"Yes! I can't wait."

He pulled back, meeting her eyes with a warm look. "No more spinning rides."

She laughed. "I told you that was from too much carnival food. I'm on salads from here on out."

He hugged her tight for a moment. "I wish I could hold you close all day, but my uncle wants me to inspect all the rides."

"Okay. I've got work to do too. You'll see me skulking around, taking pictures when no one's looking. I'm trying to capture some authenticity."

He set her on her feet and kissed her in the dizzying delicious way he had, making her forget the world. She went up on tiptoe, wrapped her arms around his neck, and pressed her body fully against his.

He broke the kiss and chuckled. "You're damn near irresistible."

"So are you! I'm addicted to your kisses."

He groaned. "Don't tell me stuff like that." He tapped the end of her nose. "Wait for tonight when I can do something about it."

"We're doing the Haunted Mansion after the Ferris wheel."

"I only get a fifteen-minute break."

She glanced across the street at the old Keller House decked out with fake spiderwebs across the porch. Nobody was in there yet. "Meet me over at the Haunted Mansion—" she pointed at the house "—once you give the all clear on the rides."

"Do you have the key?"

She laughed. "This is Fieldridge. It's either unlocked or the key is under a ceramic animal."

He gave her a slow, sexy smile. "Give me an hour."

She winked. "I'll give you two if you make it worth my while." She turned and took a step toward her purse and then yelped. He'd smacked her butt.

"Never doubt I'll make it worth your while," he said in a low, husky voice that sent ripples of tingling pleasure through her. Then he turned and swaggered back to work.

How did she get so damn lucky? She shook her head, smiling, and headed to her purse for her camera. She pulled it out and aimed the zoom lens toward Patrick checking on the kiddy ride with the circle of motorcycles. Her throat got tight, and she lowered the camera. She had gotten lucky. Both of them at a crossroads, meeting here just for the week. And what were the chances of them ever seeing each other again?

She raised the camera back to her eye and captured Patrick in his element, his white T-shirt stretching across his broad back as he worked. His movements were graceful and masculine. At least she'd have this, these pictures would be hers long after he'd moved on.

She shook off her melancholy thoughts at the sight of Sally and Mallory bickering yet seeming to light up in each other's company as they made their way to the main food stand. She waited for them to pass and then followed behind, capturing the contrast in the women's clothes and size, the way their heads often turned toward each other in rapid-fire conversation. They entertained each other with their snappy comebacks. And once they got into the kitchen in the stand, they worked in peaceful harmony, singing a seemingly unending repertoire of Johnny Cash.

She loved it. After she got her fill of pictures of that happy pair, she fluttered around the carnival, in a state of flow, the perfect frames and angles coming to her as she moved. She didn't even hear Patrick approach until he stepped directly in front of her, and his grinning face filled the frame. She snapped that picture and lowered the camera. "Has it been an hour?"

One corner of his mouth lifted. "Actually two. I had to spend a little time on the Scrambler. Anyway, it's all fixed, and I'm all yours."

She tucked her camera in her purse and took his hand. "I like the sound of that."

They practically ran to the Haunted Mansion, both of them eager to get more of what they'd started earlier. She led him around to the back door and tried the knob. Unlocked. They exchanged a grin. She stepped inside and did a quick tour of the downstairs to make sure they were alone.

"It's not that scary," Patrick said when she returned to the decorated living room.

She looked around, trying to see it as he would. As a kid, it had been terrifying, and it still gave her a little jittery feeling. Not because the coffin and cobwebs and skeletons were all that scary. It was just that it was usually dark with glowing red lights, and people tended to jump out at you at the most unexpected times. "Check out what's under that metal dome," she said, pointing to the table covered with a white tablecloth. There was always a fake bloody head under the dome, so it looked like the decapitated head was dinner.

She waited until he'd just started to lift the dome before jumping out at him with a scary, "Bwa-ha-ha!" She would've screamed bloody murder for a real good scare, but she didn't want anyone nearby to know they were inside.

He turned and cocked a brow. "You think that's scary?"

"It's terrifying at night."

"Uh-huh." He put the dome back in place and snagged her by the waist. He leaned down, his mouth brushing against her ear as he spoke. "Where should I grope you?"

"Everywhere," she breathed.

He hugged her, and she felt his laugh rumbling in his

chest. "I meant where in the house? I don't want to be interrupted."

"Oh!" She felt a little silly. "Let's go upstairs. That way if anyone comes in early, we won't be caught in our unmentionables."

He groaned.

She led him upstairs to a room decorated like a historic house should be—a bed with a handmade white quilt, an old dresser, and a variety of antiquey-looking items scattered here and there.

"We can't mess up the bed," he said. "It looks like it came with the house."

She shut the door and tried to lock it, but the old lock just kept turning and turning. Oh well. Probably no one would come in. He kicked off his shoes.

She kicked off her flip-flops too. "C'mere," she said, leaning against the door.

He closed the distance between them. "I'm so glad you're here," he said just before his lips met hers. This kiss was different, so gentle, so achingly tender that she felt tears sting her eyes. This kind of kiss was dangerous because it led to feelings that would cut deep when they went their separate ways. She needed to change things fast. She cupped him through his shorts and he sucked in a harsh breath.

And then he stared at her for a long moment. "Take off your dress."

She didn't hesitate. She quickly undid the belt and pulled it over her head. Then she flicked open her bra, dropping it to the ground, and pulled down her panties. She wanted everything with Patrick. She would never get this opportunity for passion again. She stood there naked as he took her in, his gaze heating her everywhere he looked.

"Beautiful goddess," he murmured before shedding his own clothes. He pulled a condom from his wallet and rolled it on. Then he lowered her to the floor. She wrapped her arms and legs around him, and then his mouth claimed hers—hot, urgent, demanding.

He kissed her breathless and then wrapped a hand in her

hair, tugging her head back, exposing her throat for more of his hot mouth. He nipped and tasted and sucked, and she was lost in the haze of pleasure. He dipped his head, lingering at her sensitive breasts, his mouth suckling one while his fingers rolled and tugged her other nipple. She throbbed, aching for him.

And then he shifted lower down and licked her belly button. She moaned, dimly aware that his hands were sliding to her bottom, cupping her and squeezing gently. His mouth drifted lower. "Patrick," she managed before his mouth closed over her sex and sucked hard. She cried out, shocked at the intimacy. He gentled, kissing her there with his lips and tongue. She was lost, her entire world centered on that mouth pushing her higher and higher.

"So good," he crooned. "You taste so good." Then he lowered his head again.

She gripped his hair, and he increased the pressure. Tiny gasps of pleasure escaped as her insides coiled and tightened. Close, she was so close. She panted, right on the edge of release.

"Goddess." He sucked hard and she broke, rocking helplessly against his mouth, pleasure like she'd never felt before radiating through her all the way to her toes.

He rose over her and kissed her tenderly. "So good," he murmured before spreading her legs. "Wrap your legs around me. This is gonna be a wild ride."

Her eyes flew open, and she did as he said, wrapping her legs tightly around him. He entered her slowly and then finished in a swift thrust that made her gasp. It was her first time and it stung. "Patrick," she managed.

He stilled. "You okay?"

"Give me a minute."

His fingers tightened on her hips. "I gotta move. I'll go slow."

He did, slowly pulling nearly all the way out and then a slow, deep stroke in. His mouth claimed hers, and she relaxed, taking him deeper on the next stroke. He slowly pulled out again, and her body tried to hold him, her inner muscles contracting around him.

"More," she said, and he thrust back in, bringing a rush of intense pleasure. And then she could do nothing but pant and hang on for the ride as he thrust over and over again. The only sounds their skin slapping together and their harsh pants. She dug her nails into his shoulders, which amped him up, faster, harder.

"Please," she said. That was all she could get out, but he understood, slowing down enough to slip a hand between them and stroke her sweet spot. Her entire body trembled, overwhelmed and lost in pleasure.

He dropped his hand, grabbed her ass, and thrust deep. "Now," he said harshly, thrusting again. She broke violently at the command, shuddering around him, and he followed with a guttural groan that vibrated against her neck.

He held her like that, his mouth pressed against her neck. She worked on catching her breath, her heart still pounding. That was fucking magic.

He pulled out and sat back on his knees. She stretched out her quivering legs. Wow.

"Yeah, wow," he said.

Had she said that out loud?

He flashed a smile, cupped her cheek, and kissed her tenderly. "Amazing."

She sighed a happy sigh. "We have to do a lot more of that."

"Agreed. But we should probably get out of here before they open the place up."

"Yes." She stroked a hand down his beautiful muscular chest, and he grabbed her hand.

"You don't play fair."

"Already?" she asked hopefully.

"Wouldn't take much with you." He took her hands and pulled her upright. "Get dressed."

She watched him instead, all golden skin and hard masculine perfection. He got rid of the condom, leaving it with the wrapper on the floor. "Don't let me forget that," he said.

That ass, perfection.

"Uh-huh." She watched him pull on his briefs and shorts. She really, really wanted to touch his beautiful chest again. And lick it.

"Maggie," he warned, "if you don't stop looking at me like that, I'm going to take you right up against that window so everyone can see."

She shivered and then nodded.

He groaned and tossed her bra and panties at her. "Please get dressed. You're killing me."

A laugh bubbled out. She stood, pulled her bra and panties back on, and then she just couldn't help herself—she did her happy dance. A chorus of stamping feet and then arms in the air for three leaps of joy.

Patrick froze, his hands gripping his shirt. "What was that?"

She beamed. "My happy dance. You made me happy."

"Aww, Maggie." He kissed her again and stroked her cheek. "You made me happy too."

Their gazes locked, but this time it wasn't heat radiating between them, it was pure love. An almost palpable thing in the air sparked between them. Her heart kicked up, lost in those hazel eyes. Was all this feeling coming from him? Or was it her glow building into something more?

She got a lump in her throat over all the unexpected feeling. "Patrick?" Did he feel it too? This weird and sudden turn from lust to…love?

His mouth formed a grim line. "We'll figure something out."

8

———

Maggie was reeling from the shocking feeling of mind-blowing, emotionally tangled sex. First of all, she, good girl Maggie Murphy, had had sex! And she couldn't shake the feeling that somehow she'd stumbled into love. And what did Patrick mean when he'd said, "We'll figure something out"? Was he going to figure out a way for them to be together past this one week? For how long? Where? He was moving on with his carnie family until the next part of his life began, and she was…what? Going to secretary school.

Or moving to New York City in hopes of a big break that might never come. She tensed just thinking about that. The risk seemed too high.

She stepped into the diner to meet up with the mayor's assistant, Alice, for dinner, the cheerful chatter of the locals soothing her edgy nerves.

Alice lifted a hand and summoned Maggie to her table. Maggie took a deep breath before approaching. When she got closer, she relaxed because Alice was sitting with Aunt Carolyn and some of her friends that Maggie knew too.

Aunt Carolyn shifted and pulled a chair over between her and Alice. "Have a seat."

Maggie smiled. "Thanks."

"I was telling Alice all about you," Aunt Carolyn said. "About how you starred in the high school drama club and how creative you are—"

"Thanks," Maggie interrupted. It was kind of embarrassing to have a relative praising you in front of someone as important as the mayor's assistant.

"So, Maggie, I got all the news on you," Alice said. "And I wondered if you'd like to take some pictures for some tourism brochures for Fieldridge?"

"I'd love to!" Maggie exclaimed.

"I told you," Aunt Carolyn said.

"We could pay you," Alice said. "What's your going rate?"

Her rate? She had no idea what to say.

Maggie bit her lip. "Can I get back to you on that?" She needed to ask around to find out what photographers charged. Maybe this would be a good side job while she went on auditions.

"Of course," Alice said. "But I'd like you to take pictures during the carnival. Not behind-the-scenes stuff. I mean like people having fun. Connecting, you know."

"Like the kissing booth," Aunt Carolyn put in with a devilish smile and a wink for Maggie.

"Cool," Maggie said. She couldn't find it in her to blush over kissing after what she'd done with Patrick. She didn't feel ruined. Far from it. And it hadn't felt bad or naughty either. It just felt natural. Right.

They placed their orders, and soon they were eating and chatting. Her aunt's friends were excited about an upcoming coed softball game and whether or not they should go easy on their husbands, who were getting up there in age. This caused great gales of laughter though Maggie didn't know why. Some of their husbands were late thirties. Maybe they *should* go easy on them. Her mind drifted back to Patrick. He was so much more than she'd thought he was when she'd first met him. She'd been infatuated with his prowess on the field, with his bad-boy reputation, but now...wow. Not only was he a sexual delight, he was surprisingly sweet and tender. If she wasn't careful, he'd be leaving Fieldridge with her heart. Her stomach dropped. Just the thought of Patrick leaving town made her feel ill. And she'd only spent three days with him.

Crap. Three days to fall in love. That was what the old-timers said the homebrew would do. And it really worked! She was so screwed both literally and figuratively. The worst part was, she couldn't wait to screw again. She never wanted to stop. Never, ever, ever. This was a problem.

Aunt Carolyn waved right in front of Maggie's face. "Yoo-hoo! I asked you a question."

She blinked. "What?"

"I said how's it going with your new fellow? Joe and I are big fans."

Maggie tried to smile and failed. "Oh, me too."

The group fell silent, and Maggie looked around to find the women all giving her knowing looks.

Aunt Carolyn tugged a lock of Maggie's hair. "He's special to you." It wasn't a question.

Everyone spoke at once; their questions boiling down to how serious it was with the former star football player with the bad-boy reputation.

She bit back a sigh. It was supposed to be a fun romantic carnival week. They hadn't even gotten to the fireworks, and here she was worried over the future.

"It's definitely too early to say," Maggie said, as much for them as for herself.

"Is that what he told you?" Aunt Carolyn asked.

"No," Maggie said slowly. "He said we'd figure it out. What do you think he means?" The women were all married. Maybe they had words of wisdom.

"Context," Alice said.

The women all nodded.

Maggie hesitated. *We had sex upstairs in Keller House, and things got weird at the end there* didn't seem appropriate. Especially in front of her aunt.

"Maggie?" Aunt Carolyn asked. "Come on, spill!"

Maggie winced at her aunt's enthusiasm. "I don't think I can say."

"Why not?" Aunt Carolyn asked, sounding genuinely perplexed.

The women exchanged knowing looks.

Her aunt rolled her eyes. "Come on, Maggie, just because I knew you back when you had an invisible friend? And gave you baths and—"

"Yes, that's why," Maggie interrupted before her aunt could spill anything more embarrassing. Like when she was six and streaked buck naked out the door, running in circles around the house, screaming, "I love being naked!"

"I just want to help you," Aunt Carolyn said. "You seem…distraught."

Maggie sighed. What the hell. She could really use some advice. She looked right at her aunt, willing her to read between the lines. "We danced and it was great. But after the dance there was this intense look and a strange feeling."

"Was he looking at you intensely or the other way around?" Alice asked.

"Both," Maggie replied. "We were sort of in an *after-dance* moment. I couldn't look away because there was so much unexpected—" she had to swallow over the lump in her throat "—emotion. I don't know if it was me or him or both, but it was intense." She heard someone let out a happy sigh before she finished with the most confusing part. "And I said, 'Patrick?' and he said, 'We'll figure it out.'"

"My little Maggie is in love!" Aunt Carolyn declared.

She felt herself flush even as some part of her knew, deep down, that all this feeling must be more than lust and intense like. But it was truly the worst timing ever.

Maggie stared at the table. "I never planned for this to happen."

The women laughed, and Maggie snapped her head up. What the hell? They were laughing at her?

"We're laughing with you, I swear!" Aunt Carolyn said. "No one plans when they fall in love. Timing is always a roll of the dice."

"It's too soon, too fast," Maggie said. "I don't know where I'm going to end up. He's a carnie for now. He's still trying to figure out where he's going to end up."

"Do you want to stay in Fieldridge?" her aunt asked, her expression hopeful.

"You know I love it here," Maggie replied honestly. "But I'm considering other options—"

"You could move in with me," Aunt Carolyn offered. It was sweet, but her aunt was happily married. She'd feel like she'd be intruding on their little family. Definitely a third wheel there.

"Thanks, but I wouldn't want to intrude," Maggie said.

"What's Patrick want to do now that he graduated?" Aunt Carolyn asked.

Maggie sighed. "He doesn't know. He's still upset about the end of his football career."

"Maybe he could work with Joe in the auto repair shop," Aunt Carolyn offered. "He's been working on carnival rides, so he must know machinery. Joe could train him. He could be based in Fieldridge. Say the word and I'll set it up."

Maggie stared at her aunt, her brain whirling with that possibility. Would Patrick like working on cars? Based in Fieldridge? Maybe they could get married and get a little place together. Whoa. What was she thinking? No guy wanted anything that heavy after just a few nights together. She'd never been in such a strange confusing head space. She usually just went with the flow, flying by the seat of her pants. Everything suddenly felt too much. Too intense.

"Take a deep breath," Aunt Carolyn said. "You don't have to figure it all out tonight. Just enjoy each other."

Maggie flushed. She went back to her meal, feeling surprisingly included with her aunt's friends. These ladies were right. She should just enjoy her time with Patrick.

Alice checked her watch. "Six thirty. I have to go."

Maggie stood too. She was supposed to meet Patrick on his break soon. "Thanks for dinner and the lovely company. I have to go too. I've got an appointment with a Ferris wheel."

Aunt Carolyn made kissy noises. "You know, if you kiss a girl on the Ferris wheel, that means you're going steady."

The women laughed, and Maggie made her escape.

~

Patrick never thought the Ferris wheel was anything special. Just a slow up-and-down ride. Pretty boring, actually, but now knowing Maggie was going to be with him, that they'd be kissing, now he was excited. But also nervous. He wiped his clammy hands on the front of his shorts. Something weird had happened after the most amazing sex of his life. It hadn't been his first time, but it had been the first time with that kind of intensity. They'd looked in each other's eyes and it felt like she held his heart in her hands. Like he'd never again be able to give it to anyone else and could only pray she wouldn't damage it.

Crazy. That was crazy.

It must've been lust combined with…friendly like. Intense like, yes, but that had to be all it was. They'd only known each other three days. Except for that one night at the Valentine's Day dance. Maggie must've planted that falling-for-each-other idea in his head when she told him about the homebrew superstition. He wasn't superstitious. Well, at least not about women.

He paced back and forth, waiting for her, and then finally there she was. His heart kicked up just at the sight of her. She'd changed into a white and red striped dress, with skinny straps, that ended mid-thigh. It suited her perfectly. Bare legs in beige heels. *Mine.*

He closed the distance between them, grabbed her in a big hug, and swung her around like he'd wanted to do from the first moment they met because she was so petite. She squealed and laughed. He set her down slowly, letting her body slide down the front of his.

She searched his expression. "That was some welcome."

He bit back his immediate reply, *I missed you,* and went

with the much cooler, "I'm playing up the romantic carnival bit."

She went up on tiptoe and kissed him gently. "I like it. Now, let me just get this out of the way. There was kind of a serious moment back at the Haunted Mansion, and I think we should just focus on having fun this week."

He cupped her bare shoulders, reveling in the smooth soft skin. "No problem." And as soon as he figured out how they could have a real future together, he'd have no problem with that too.

"To the Ferris wheel!"

He grabbed her hand, entwined his fingers with hers, and headed over to the ride. "So from what I could tell, it seems the thing to do is make out at the top."

"Or at the bottom," she said, grinning mischievously.

"Isn't the point that you feel like it's a private moment?"

Her lips curved in a sexy little smile. "I just want to kiss you a lot."

"You don't care if we put on a show?"

"Nope. I really don't. Because this is my first romantic carnival, and I'm going to enjoy it."

He stopped short. "What do you mean your first romantic carnival? I thought you were from here."

"I am. I just never went to the carnival with a date."

"Never?"

"Never," she said quietly.

That was when he remembered her Kooky Maggie nickname and how maybe the guys around here hadn't appreciated her like they should have.

He cupped her cheek and spoke near her ear. "I'm so honored to be your first romantic carnival date."

She pulled back and looked directly in his eyes. "I thought I knew you from football, but the real Patrick is so much more than passes caught, yards run, touchdowns scored. Wow. Just wow. I'm honored you let me see that."

He couldn't breathe for a moment. He couldn't believe she just said that. Nobody thought of who he was underneath and definitely not without football. If anything, they thought he was trailer trash. He pulled her close, tucking her head against his chest so she wouldn't see the annoying wetness in his eyes.

"Hey, lovebirds," his uncle called, walking past in his clown outfit complete with a rainbow wig, full makeup, red polka-dotted romper, and giant red shoes. His uncle had been working on his balloon-animal skills this summer, and Patrick had picked it up too.

"Hey," Patrick called.

Maggie turned with a smile and squeaked. "He's a clown," she said under her breath. She raised a hand, and his uncle honked a giant horn at her and continued on his way.

"Yeah," Patrick said, taking her hand and continuing to the Ferris wheel.

"That's terrifying," she said with a shudder. "Clowns are creepy."

He laughed. "I think your idea of terrifying needs work. The Haunted Mansion wasn't terrifying, and my uncle as a clown giving little kids balloon animals is definitely not terrifying."

"It is, trust me."

"I do the balloon animals too."

She stopped short, eyes wide. "Tell me you don't dress like a clown."

He didn't, but he saw an opportunity. "Patricky the clown! Woo-woo!" He did a few funny ape movements and then feinted like he was going to grab her.

She yelped and ran away. He chased her to the Ferris wheel, caught her easily around the waist, and wrapped her in his arms. "Aww, Maggie, you please me." He used her funny turn of phrase.

She cracked up and looked at him over her shoulder. "Same here, trust me."

He gave her a quick kiss. "Come on. We're carnies, Robert will let us go ahead of the line. He knows I've only got a short break."

"What happens if you're late?"

"Mallory will chew me out. She's working the games for me, and she prefers the food stand."

"Okay. Let's do it."

What did it say about him that his cock stirred at the words? He was like a sex addict around her. Geez, they just did it earlier today.

They approached Robert and were ushered onto the next car. Maggie put their seatbelt on, put her purse in the mesh pocket in front of them, and settled back, leaning against his side. He slid an arm around her shoulders.

She swung her feet back and forth. "I can't believe I'm riding the Ferris wheel with Patrick O'Hare."

"I can't believe I'm riding the Ferris wheel with a goddess."

She turned to him, her eyes full of warmth and something that looked like wonder. "I'm so lucky," she whispered. And before he could say the same, her lips met his. He speared his fingers through her hair, cupping her head and deepening the kiss. She opened immediately, and he thrust his tongue inside, tasting cherries and sex. He wanted her so freaking bad, but they were on a ride. He had to put everything into the kiss. She must've agreed, because the kiss turned wild. Their tongues tangled, mouths fused together, her hands were all over him, tunneling through his hair, sliding over his shoulders and then over his chest. He kept his hands on her head, his fingers tightening in her hair, the other hand on her jaw, holding her in place for more. She nipped his bottom lip then ran her tongue over it. He groaned.

She broke the kiss so suddenly he felt disoriented. "Is this the top?" she asked.

He looked around. "Almost." He leaned in for more.

"Wait," she said. "I want to know what it feels like at the very top with the whole carnival underneath us, the view of Fieldridge, the lights, the people. Ooh! I need my camera!"

She grabbed her purse from the mesh holder in front of them, pulled out the camera, and started snapping pictures. Damn. Guess she wasn't feeling it like he was. But then she grabbed his shirt and pulled him in while holding the camera up, aimed at them. "Kiss me," she said.

He brushed his lips across hers gently, not wanting to look like the sex-crazed animal he was on film. She ran her tongue over his bottom lip and then into his mouth, and he forgot about the camera, cupping her by the back of the neck and deepening the kiss. She made those little noises in the back of her throat that made him crazy. He couldn't stop kissing her.

When he finally let her up for air, she looked dazed. He liked that he got to her as much as she got to him.

"What are you going to do with those pictures of us kissing?" he asked. He hoped it wasn't for the flyer.

She stroked his hair and gazed into his eyes. "Treasure them."

He didn't know what to say. She overwhelmed him in the best possible way. She turned and took in the view of the town and the lit-up carnival and the people. And he took in the view of her.

It was the best damn fifteen-minute break of his life.

And then it was over.

He got off the ride, still holding her hand, and then pulled her in close, wrapping his arms around her waist. "Stop by tonight at ten. That's when I get off."

"You sure will," she said, her blue eyes full of mischief and fun.

He grinned. "And tomorrow night I'm free for the fireworks."

"Yes!"

"And I want to see you the next night, and the next, and the next."

Her voice came out small. "When do you leave?"

"Monday morning."

She brightened. "So that's six more nights."

It wasn't enough, but it was something. Six nights to figure out how to keep Maggie in his life. "I hope we can take the inner-tube ride together a little longer than that," he said.

"Me too. We'll help each other navigate the river of uncertainty."

"That sounds real good." He stroked her hair. "Hopefully we'll meet up at the end once we both know where we're heading."

She cocked her head. "Wait, what did we just decide?"

"I want more than a week with you." Much, much more.

"Yes."

They sealed it with a kiss.

And then went their separate ways. But some part of him knew it wouldn't be that easy.

9

Aunt Carolyn must've gotten in her head because when Maggie got off that Ferris wheel, she felt like she and Patrick were going steady. Okay, so they were only seeing each other for the week exclusively. How difficult was a week of exclusive dating anyway? But somehow the kiss on the ride took things to a deeper level. And all that talk about meeting up once they knew what they were doing in their respective careers had been very, very promising.

After Patrick went back to work, Maggie wandered around the carnival in a state of bliss, taking pictures for the carnival and the Fieldridge tourism brochure. For a small town, it really could be a fun destination for tourists, with all of the parades, carnivals, and dances. She got some pictures of Patrick working the basketball game, encouraging little kids to stand a little closer and handing over big teddy bear prizes with a smile.

Her heart squeezed.

It wasn't just the gorgeous face and gorgeous body, his exciting bad-boy rep. Now that she knew him, she saw his tender side, his open acceptance of other people with no judgment. He was gorgeous inside and out. Damn, she'd gone and done it. Falling for Patrick in the middle of a tumultuous time in both their lives.

She spent the next day in her basement darkroom, developing the first crop of pictures. She wanted to hear Odd Todd's opinion on her work before she took more. Oh, Patrick, you beautiful man. Every shot with him was gorgeous. She really had it bad.

By the time she finished, she only had an hour before she needed to meet up with Patrick for the fireworks. She left the pictures to dry and hurried upstairs. Time for fun.

She got ready, wearing her favorite purple and pink diamond-patterned sundress. The fabric was a soft cotton that was super comfortable and flattered her petite figure rather than hiding it. She took off her panties, deciding to make fooling around as easy as possible for Patrick. No bra either. Now who was the rebel badass?

A short while later, Patrick pulled up to her house in his uncle's truck. This time he walked inside and met her parents. She couldn't help her smile. It meant he took their relationship seriously. Her parents were polite.

"Bye!" she called, hurrying out the door with Patrick. She figured if the park was too crowded with other couples, they could drive to a secluded spot and make good use of the truck bed. Or better yet, spread out a blanket on the ground near some trees for a private oasis. Damn, she was good at all this clandestine sex stuff, considering how her previous experience was limited to a bedroom in a haunted house. Something about Fieldridge in the summer made sex outdoors under a starry sky oh-so-appealing. Or maybe that was Patrick.

Speaking of the man who rocked her world, he opened the passenger-side door of the truck for her and grinned. "Hey, goddess, ready to go all the way?"

She smiled back. "I'm not wearing panties, so yeah."

He made a weird choking sound, and she laughed, pleased that she'd topped him in the sexual-suggestion game.

"Cool," he said in a strangled voice.

She climbed into the truck. As soon as they'd pulled out towards the park, she said, "I've been thinking more about doing the photography thing as a side job while I look for acting jobs. I'm doing some work for the mayor's office too."

"Wow. That was fast. You've already got two clients in a week. So would you stay in Fieldridge and commute for auditions?"

"I'm thinking about it. I do love it here. Though it would be a real pain to commute." The trip to the city was an hour and a half by car, more by train with connections. And she didn't have the money for a car.

They were quiet for a few moments.

She broke the silence. "The question is, can I keep bringing in new photography clients? I've never really tried to run my own business."

"You could learn that stuff. My uncle could probably help you too. The carnival has been his own business for years."

"Okay. Thank you." She wanted to suggest he stay in Fieldridge too and work for Joe in his repair shop, but some part of her felt it was too much too soon, so she backed off.

"I've started running again," Patrick said.

"Really?"

"Yeah. I mean, I know I'm not in training anymore, but I feel better when I work out. I'm used to a really intense physical regimen. I'm going to start lifting weights again, building muscle. It just feels good to use my body like that, to really push myself."

"Patrick, that's wonderful!"

"Thanks. I might try another sport. Just for fun."

"You totally should." He was an athlete, still young enough to excel at a lot of sports.

"We'll see. First I need to get back in shape."

"You never got out of shape," she replied, squeezing his bicep.

He chuckled. "I used to be much more in shape, but thanks."

They got to the park and found the field for the fireworks viewing was already pretty crowded. He turned to her, a clear lusty question in his eyes. "I've got a plan B," she said.

"Blanket in a private spot just beyond those trees or the back of the truck."

"Private spot sounds good to me."

She grabbed the blanket and guided him through a copse of trees where they could have some privacy. Most people would be watching the fireworks in the opposite direction from them. Perfect.

They settled on the blanket, lying side by side. Patrick spoke up. "If you stay in Fieldridge, maybe I could find work here too. Something better than working for the market."

She felt breathless at the idea. It was what she wanted, for them to keep seeing each other, but was it really what he wanted? If so, why was he traveling with his uncle's carnival instead of working in town right now?

"Do you actually want to work here?" she asked.

He hesitated before finally stroking her hair and saying, "I want to be with you."

"I want to be with you too," she said, "but I want you to be happy. We're talking about your future job. If you're not happy, you'll feel stuck."

He rolled to his back and threw his arm over his forehead. "I know it's not ideal, but it's all I could come up with. Without football—"

"What do you think about working on machines like in an auto repair shop?"

He propped up on one elbow. "That's specific."

She laughed. Now that she knew he really wanted to keep seeing her, she felt okay about bringing it up. "My uncle would be willing to train you, and you could work in his shop. You're good at machinery."

"It's kind of perfect, actually," he said. "I've fixed cars before too."

"I can set it up with my uncle."

"Okay. I'm definitely interested." He pulled her close, wrapping her in his arms. He whispered in her ear, "If I make Fieldridge my home base, will you be at home waiting for me?"

"You mean a home together?" she whispered.

He pulled back to look in her eyes. "Yes," he said solemnly.

"Yes," she replied just as solemnly.

They grinned at each other. Then she launched herself at him, rolling on top of him and covering him with kisses. "I love you!" she exclaimed.

He went stock-still.

Crap. Maybe she shouldn't have—

"I love you too," he said in a husky voice before rolling her under him. He kissed her tenderly, reverently, and they made love under the stars, absorbed in their own fireworks.

Patrick was feeling content for the first time in a long time. He'd met with Joe this morning, and the job was his if he wanted it. He headed back to the trailer he shared with his uncle to tell him the good news. He wasn't there, but his uncle had left a note that Patrick's mom had said someone had called for him. He didn't recognize the number.

He returned the call, curious.

"Is this Patrick O'Hare?" a gravelly voice asked.

"Yes."

"This is Coach Gary McDonald with the New York Titans."

Patrick nearly lost his footing. That was the team he'd tried out for and hadn't made the cut. "Yes, hello, Coach. How are you?"

The coach laughed, a rusty sound. "I'm fine, son. I'm calling because Darryl Thomas destroyed his knee and he's out for the year. How do you feel about joining us for training camp in August?"

Patrick's mind spun with the possibilities. Daryl was their wide receiver, and a damn good one too. He couldn't believe it. He hadn't missed his chance. Hadn't missed his dream after all.

"Son?"

"Yes!"

"All right then. It was close between you and Darryl in tryouts, but now we'd like to take a chance on you. It will be intense. We have to prove ourselves as a new team. Can you hold up under that kind of pressure?"

His mind flashed to when he'd screwed up at the state championship, hurting over Sandra. Never again. "I can. The Titans will have my absolute focus."

"Well, now, we'll see, won't we?"

"With all due respect, sir, my last season I had seven hundred fifty receiving yards—"

The coach barked out a laugh. "Now that's the fighting spirit I like to hear. Camp starts August first. I'll mail you the papers."

"Thank you, sir."

"Looking forward to seeing what you can do for the Titans, Handsy."

"Patrick."

"Yup. Bye."

Patrick hung up and did a fist pump. "Yes!" He ran to the carnival grounds to find his uncle when it suddenly hit him that he had two pieces of good news, two opportunities, and he could only choose one.

Of course he had to choose football. He already had. Football had always been his dream.

But Maggie wanted to stay here in Fieldridge. He couldn't bring her to training camp. It wasn't even a definite he'd be on the team. They could still cut him loose at the end of August when training camp ended. Even if he did get a contract with the Titans, his life would be on the road, playing in stadiums all over the country, living in hotels and buses. Hopefully for the next ten years or more.

He slowed his steps. He could always see Maggie in the off-season, right? But he knew it would be hard. Football would become his life.

What was fair to her?

He went for a run, hoping the activity would help him think through the problem, but by the time he finished, nothing was clear. He'd been handed a rare do-over. He'd told himself if he ever got the chance again, he'd focus one hundred percent on football. His focus was already split, though, because he'd fallen for Maggie. This was where he should cut ties. This was where he had to sacrifice for football. Falling for Sandra and the subsequent heartbreak had nearly destroyed his dream. It would be so much worse if that happened with Maggie down the road. Now that his dream was within reach, he couldn't risk another fumble.

Dammit. Why couldn't he have met Maggie after he'd made something of himself? He knew it wasn't fair to ask her to wait around for that to happen. He looked up at the Ferris wheel, remembering how excited and happy Maggie was to have her first carnival kiss at the top with him. He couldn't bear to look over at the Haunted Mansion, remembering the time they'd had there. This should be the happiest day of his life, and instead he was all twisted up and confused. Maybe his uncle could help him figure stuff out.

He found him sitting on a fold-out chair in front of a trailer, staring in the distance. "Guess who just quit?" Uncle Todd asked.

"Who?"

"Our jazz polka cowboy."

"Really? Why?"

"Got invited to join a jazz polka band back in Pittsburgh."

Patrick took a long swallow of water. "That's a thing?"

"Apparently."

"You don't sound too torn up about it."

"He wasn't that popular, and it saves us on payroll. He was only with us a couple of seasons. Anyway, his trailer's free, so…if you want it, for you and Maggie, we'd love to have her with us for the rest of the season."

Patrick sat on his haunches next to his uncle. "That's generous. Thank you."

"It's nothing. We all like her." His uncle grinned, the light reflecting off the diamond T in his gold tooth. "Whenever she's around, you get big love-puppy eyes just like Tramp."

Unfortunately, Patrick knew exactly what his uncle meant from that scene in *Lady and the Tramp*. He must look like a dope half the time he was around Maggie. "I just had big news." He took a deep breath. "The New York Titans want me at training camp."

His uncle was silent. Patrick glanced over to see his uncle deep in concentration. "Sorry," Uncle Todd said. "Never heard of them."

"They're a new team." At his uncle's blank look, he added, "A pro team. Their wide receiver is injured, and they want me to take his place."

"Wow! That's great!"

Patrick grinned. "Thanks."

"Wait, what happens when their other wide receiver gets better?" Patrick had thought of that too, but the bench wasn't deep. Hopefully they could both have a place on the team.

"I guess we'll both play. That's up to the coach. He can play three wide receivers on the field at the same time." His uncle didn't follow football at all. He only knew touchdowns.

"So you're on the team?"

Patrick straightened. "If I prove myself at training camp, chances are good I'll be on the team. For now, no contract."

His uncle put a hand on his shoulder. "Why aren't you jumping for joy?"

Patrick blew out a breath. "I'm not sure what to do about Maggie."

"What do you mean?"

"I mean I don't want to hurt her, but I need to focus on football. You know how I lost focus before over Sandra."

"It wasn't just her. You had a lot going on, trying to help out when your mom was so sick." His mom had gotten a bad flu that landed her in the hospital.

He dipped his head. "I should've powered through."

"You've got heart. That's what makes you a good player."

That was also what made him a bad player. He'd learned his lesson the hard way. The only way for him to keep focused on football was to push all that emotional stuff down.

Patrick grunted. "I'm going to hit the shower." He was soaked with sweat from his run.

"I know you'll make a good choice," his uncle said, which made Patrick feel ten times worse.

He reminded himself he'd really only known Maggie less than a week. They probably wouldn't have gotten in so deep if they both hadn't been at a point in their lives where they felt lost. They shared an inner tube in the river of uncertainty. That was all. Now he needed to get off the ride. He had a definite goal—one that required strict discipline to training. They should just go their separate ways when the carnival left town on Monday. Yes, it would hurt. But they'd both get over it and move on to where they were supposed to be in their lives. He wouldn't ask her to be a backup plan to football in case things didn't work out with the Titans; he had to be all in with her or not at all. All in with football or not at all. It all made perfect logical sense.

So why was his gut churning over just the thought of dimming her sunny smile?

10

———

Maggie spent the day working on the carnival flyers. She wanted to have everything ready before the carnies left Field-ridge. And she really wanted to get Odd Todd's opinion on a few variations. Alice had loved the pictures she'd taken for the tourism brochure. When all was said and done, Maggie felt like she could be happy here at home as a freelance photographer. Maybe a big part of that was being with Patrick, but still. She could always commute to the city for auditions, even though it was a bear of a commute. A niggling worry that she didn't know much about the business side of things nagged at her, but she pushed that down. She'd talk to people who did know that stuff. And she'd figure it out somehow.

She couldn't wait to see Patrick tonight after his shift and hear all about his meeting with Joe. It felt almost too good to be true that she and Patrick had found each other and fallen in love, but she wasn't the kind of person to overthink things. What they had felt right. That was enough for her.

Only when she found Patrick coming off his shift working the kiddy motorcycle ride, he didn't seem all that happy to see her. He didn't smile or call her goddess, and when she kissed him, his return kiss was a quick peck before he pulled away.

"You want to go for a drive?" she asked. She'd been hoping they could drive out to a field and "dance" under the stars.

"We need to talk," he said, indicating a bench nearby.

Maggie shivered though it was still warm. Why did she suddenly feel like her happy little bubble was about to pop? The carnival was getting that ghost town feel again, as the food stand was shuttered, the lights shut down, and workers covered game prizes with tarps.

Patrick took her hand and pulled her along. "Come on."

She sat cross-legged on the bench next to him. "What is it?"

"I got called for training camp with a new football team, the New York Titans."

"Oh, Patrick, that's great news!" She threw her arms around him in a big hug. "I'm so happy for you!"

"Thanks."

She pulled back. "Why aren't you excited?"

"I am. Believe me. It's just—" he looked off in the distance "—football is, like, everything to me."

"I know. It's like a dream come true."

"I have to keep my head in the game. You know?" He still wasn't looking at her. She got a really bad feeling in the pit of her stomach. Of course he had to think of the game in order to be a good player. Where was he going with this?

"Handsy! There you are!" a feminine voice called.

They both turned to see a gorgeous statuesque blonde woman approaching in a tight sleeveless red dress and red stilettos. Maggie sucked in a breath. Sandra Westwood. Patrick's ex-girlfriend.

"Sandra," Patrick said under his breath, standing and crossing to the woman.

Maggie stood too, wondering if she should join them and introduce herself or hang back for a bit.

But then Sandra threw herself in Patrick's arms and kissed him passionately. Maggie blinked. Patrick pushed her away gently.

She swallowed over the lump in her throat, her eyes hot.

Was this what he wanted to talk about? That he was getting back together with Sandra? Maybe Sandra was his football good-luck charm. She had been there when he had such a great season. Maybe he'd called Sandra after he got the news that he had a future in football after all.

Her heart raced. They were speaking in a low tone that she couldn't hear. Part of her wanted to bolt, and part of her wanted to slap them both. She took a deep breath and approached just in time to hear Sandra say, "I never should've left you. I'm so sorry. I still love you. Can you forgive me?"

"Hi," Maggie said, standing next to Patrick. "I'm Maggie."

Patrick was quiet, and Maggie's heart lodged in her throat. Why wasn't he setting Sandra straight? Why wasn't he putting his arm around Maggie or *something* to show that he actually cared about her?

Sandra's eyes narrowed as she looked Maggie up and down, taking in her favorite cheery yellow blouse and blue capris with a look of disgust. "Is it serious, Handsy?"

"It's Patrick," he said. "And we've only been together a week."

Maggie's gut twisted. Patrick had said he loved her, and she'd believed him. What was she? Just a fun time until something better came along? Like football? Or Sandra?

Sandra wrapped herself around Patrick's arm, pressing her breasts against his bicep. She gave Maggie a fake smile. "Patrick and I were together for three months."

"Two," Patrick said, extricating his arm from Sandra. He turned to Maggie. "I had no idea she'd be here."

"We're in love," Sandra said. "Say goodbye, Handsy."

Patrick gritted his teeth. "How did you find me?"

Sandra lifted one shoulder. "I have my ways."

"What about J.J.?" he asked. J.J. McTavish was the former quarterback of the Bobcats. Last Maggie heard, J.J. was playing for the New England Blazers.

Sandra frowned. "J.J. is a prick. As soon as he got to Boston, he went out one time with the team and told me the guys said it's better to be single when you're pro. I'm sure that's not true. There's lots of football wives. You don't feel that way, do you?"

"I don't know," Patrick muttered.

Maggie spoke up. "Patrick?"

He took Maggie to the side and spoke in a low voice. "I need to talk to her first, and then you and I will talk. Trust me, it's the fastest way to get rid of her. She loves drama."

Maggie got the message loud and clear. She was second choice.

"Don't bother," she said before turning on her heel and walking away. Patrick didn't say a word. But Sandra spoke loud enough for the entire town to hear.

"Ooh, Handsy, a kissing booth! Let's go try it out!"

Maggie kept going. The kissing booth was empty right now. She didn't dare look back to see if they were heading that way. She headed straight to the diner, wanting nothing more than to drown her sorrows in ice cream.

When she got to the diner, it was crowded with people. She took a stool at the counter and ordered up a sundae with extra hot fudge. She dove in, wallowing in sugary misery.

The waitress pointed down the other end of the counter. "Your sundae is on him."

She looked over. Quinn, the singing corn dog man. He was thirtyish with short black hair and blue eyes, tall and muscular. Sweetly sexy. The kind of guy who would never dump her the minute he got promoted to a bigger corn dog stand. He grinned, and she gestured for him to join her.

Quinn appeared at her side. "Where's Patrick?" he sang in his deep voice near her ear. She got a hot shiver. The man should be on the radio.

"He's with Sandra." She frowned and took another spoonful.

"She crushed his heart," Quinn sang. "I don't believe he'd go back."

"Quinn?"

"Hmm?"

"I love your voice. It's gorgeous, like you should be on the radio or something." He smiled, so she went on with what she knew was a touchy subject. "I know the singing has been working for you, but have you tried speaking since you tried the singing?"

He shook his head, serious now.

"Can you try for me?"

"I've been singing for two years," he sang on a down note. His voice dropped even lower. "What should I say?"

"Whatever you want." She smiled encouragingly.

He smiled back, his blue eyes lighting up. "Would you like to dance?" he sang.

"Say it, not sing it."

He nodded and cleared his throat. "Maggie..." He spoke her name beautifully.

"Yes?" she said with a big smile.

"Would you like to dance?" he asked with no hint of a stutter.

They grinned at each other. She was so darn proud of him for having the courage to try that she took him up on it. "Sure."

Patrick watched Maggie bolt in the direction of the diner and immediately wanted to follow, but Sandra was pulling his arm, demanding they talk, so he figured he'd better get rid of her first. He'd been taken by surprise with the kiss she'd laid on him. She'd always been aggressive, but she also knew how to satisfy a guy, so he'd never complained. Now that he'd been with Maggie, he could see the difference between Sandra's almost completely one-sided way of making love and the fun of two people who loved each other coming together. Oh, fuck. He did love Maggie. What the hell was he doing pushing her away?

Football, you idiot. You have to choose football. All in. One hundred percent focus. The proof was right in front of him.

"Handsy," Sandra cooed, "it's so good to see you again!"

"Stop calling me Handsy. It's Patrick." She would never

call him Patrick no matter how many times he'd asked. Even when they got naked. She only wanted him to be that guy—the football player.

She pouted and ran her hand up and down his bicep. "But that's your name. You're good with those hands."

He took in a deep breath and let it out. He'd been raised to be respectful of women, but Sandra was irritating the frick out of him. "Have a seat. We'll talk." He gestured to the bench where he'd been about to bail on Maggie. He had to hurry this up so he could apologize to Maggie. The look on her face when she saw him with Sandra had just about killed him. He needed her to know that he and Sandra were never happening again.

Sandra didn't take a seat. Instead she wrapped her arms around his neck and pressed her body fully against his. "I missed you," she said in a breathy sexy voice. The one that used to have him ripping her clothes off.

He tried to pull her arms off him, but she clung to him. "I want to talk," he said, gently pushing her away. "Over on that bench."

"Fine," she said on a sigh.

She took his hand and walked with him to the bench. As soon as he sat down, she sat in his lap. He lifted her and set her back on the bench. "I know why you were with me before," he said, "and I know why you want to be with me now. It won't work. I don't want to be with someone who just wants me for football."

"I don't just want you for football. I love you."

Did she really? Because he had really loved her before. He didn't want to hurt her feelings. But wait…

"Is that why you dumped me as soon as J.J. got a big offer?" he asked.

"J.J. came on to me," she said. "He really poured it on with the flowers and love notes."

Patrick's brows drew together. He couldn't imagine J.J. writing love notes. His teammate was rough, crude, and cursed a blue streak.

Sandra rushed on. "I was confused. But he showed his

true colors and…" She blinked rapidly and a single tear tracked down one cheek. "I realized how good I had it with you."

He pressed his lips together. He wasn't sure if she was faking or not, but that tear seemed real. Just in case she was serious, he let her down gently. "I need to focus one hundred percent on football. I can't be with anyone right now."

"Not even that weird red-haired girl?"

He stood abruptly, biting back the blast he wanted to level in her direction for calling Maggie weird. *Enough.* He had to talk to Maggie. "Goodbye, Sandra."

"Will you call me when you get settled on the team? I'll wait for you."

She sounded sincere. He'd never ask someone to wait around for him to hit the big time. She stood and hooked her fingers in the belt loop of his jeans, pulling him close.

He looked down at her beautiful face. One look at the cold, calculating look in those blue eyes told him everything he needed to know. Maybe he had a bit of his uncle's gift for knowing someone with a look in their eyes. "If I don't make the team, should I still call?" Not that he ever wanted to be with her again. But he wanted to hear her say it. To admit that she only ever wanted him for football.

She laughed, a hard, fake-sounding laugh. "Of course you'll make the team! Don't be silly."

"What if I don't? Would you still want to be with me?"

She hesitated.

"Thanks, I've got my answer." He strode away, determined to find Maggie and finish their talk.

"Handsy, wait!" Sandra called.

He turned. "Go find some other football player to follow to the big time."

"But I want you!"

He winced. "I'm sorry. I can't."

Her face fell. He kept walking, and he didn't hear her heels clicking behind him. Even though she'd broken his heart before, he didn't want to hurt her any more than he had to. He got no pleasure in revenge. He needed to see Maggie and explain as nicely as possible that it was over. He had to be all in with football. It wasn't personal. He wouldn't be with anyone. Bachelor Patrick. All in, Coach.

He'd just about convinced himself of the necessity of his bachelor state by the time he reached the diner. And then he opened the door, took one look at Maggie dancing in Quinn's arms, and everything went to hell.

11

Maggie was having a blast dancing with Quinn. They'd shifted to an open area by the jukebox and he'd led her in a sweet waltz. Quinn spun her around and then dipped her suddenly over his knee before slowly pulling her back up and gazing into her eyes. She was breathless, caught up in the expert way he moved. She'd never had such a good dance partner before. She opened her mouth to tell him so when a large hand grabbed Quinn by the collar and yanked him away.

"Patrick!" Maggie exclaimed. "Let go of him!"

Patrick was in Quinn's face, still gripping Quinn's shirt. "Back off," Patrick growled.

Quinn simply stared, showing no fear. He'd known Patrick for years, and maybe that meant he knew Patrick wouldn't actually kick his ass.

"Patrick?" she asked.

He spared her a quick glance. "What?"

"You interrupted our dance. You'll have to wait your turn." She pulled Quinn back to her, and he took the lead again, away from Patrick.

"What the hell!" Patrick yelled.

"And you have to ask nicely," she called over her shoulder before Quinn shifted her away.

"Told you," Quinn said with a sigh.

He had. He'd told her Patrick would follow her here, though she'd seriously doubted it with the beautiful Sandra all over him. Quinn even predicted that Patrick would try to cut in on their dance. As Quinn explained, Sandra was a football groupie, and Patrick had seen her true colors months ago. Still, she was kinda happy to see Patrick jealous. That meant he cared.

The door to the diner banged open. "Handsy!" Sandra shouted, drawing everyone's attention.

Patrick went to her, and Sandra wrapped her arms around his neck, pressing herself against him. And now Maggie was jealous. Which she was less happy about. Patrick was trying to push Sandra away, but the woman clung to him.

Quinn chuckled. "We should trade partners."

"You're too good for her," Maggie spat.

"No, I'm not," Quinn replied darkly. Her eyes snapped to his. She read pain there, and then just as quickly his expression shuttered closed.

"All right," Maggie said.

They stopped next to Patrick and Sandra in the entryway. Patrick had managed to put some space between them.

Quinn made an elaborate sweeping bow in front of Sandra before singing in a deep bass voice, "May I have this dance?"

Sandra's jaw dropped.

Quinn grinned and took her hand.

"No, wait," Sandra said, grabbing for Patrick, but he'd already stepped away.

Patrick took Maggie's hand and led her out the door. "We need to talk."

She glanced over her shoulder to see Quinn leading Sandra in a fast-paced dance with lots of spins and dips. She stifled a laugh and followed Patrick outside.

Patrick leaned down to whisper in her ear, "I'm not with Sandra, and I never will be."

"Why'd you let her kiss you?"

"She surprised me."

She looked in the diner, where Sandra was now sitting at

the counter with Quinn. Sandra was watching Patrick while Quinn watched Sandra.

Maggie turned back to Patrick. "She wants you back."

"She can't have me."

"You ditched me," she said, trying to keep the emotion from her voice. She felt like howling.

"You're the one who walked away," Patrick said. "Then I see you with Quinn."

"It was a dance," she snapped. "He's my friend. And I thought I was your girlfriend, and then all you have to say is we've only been together for a week."

He threw his hands up. "We have only been together for a week!"

"Whatever you say," she muttered. She stalked off.

"Get back here!" Patrick demanded, following her.

"You can't leave me here!" Sandra hollered, rushing out of the diner.

Quinn followed Sandra.

Great.

The four of them just stood there in the quiet parking lot for a moment. Patrick looked to Maggie, who looked to Quinn, who looked to Sandra.

Sandra put her hands on her hips and looked back at Quinn. "And what do you do?"

Quinn stiffened. "Wh-what do you th-think I do?" At the reappearance of his stutter, Maggie went to his side in support.

Sandra's lip curled. "Wh-what do you th-think I do?" she mimicked. "Nice stutter."

"Sandra!" Patrick exclaimed.

Quinn's blank stare back at Sandra was unnerving. Like he'd checked out.

Maggie wedged herself between Sandra and Quinn and glared at Sandra. "I don't like the way you're talking to my friend."

"And I don't like you, freak," Sandra spat. She grabbed Maggie by the hair.

"Ah!" Maggie screamed. It felt like Sandra was pulling her hair out by the roots.

Patrick grabbed Sandra's fingers and peeled her off. Sandra lunged again, and Patrick had to hold her back, wrapping his arms around her from behind. Sandra gave Maggie a little victory smile. Bitch.

"Ladies," Quinn sang, "no need to fight over me. My heart's taken." And with that, he strolled off into the night, whistling.

Patrick shoved Sandra away. "I never want to see you again."

Sandra looked shocked. "What? Just because that guy had a stutter? I love you!"

"I don't love you," Patrick said.

"Yes, you do! You did. I know you could again!"

Even Maggie cringed at how pathetic Sandra sounded.

"It's over," Patrick said harshly.

"Because of her?" Sandra spat.

"Because of you," Patrick said.

Sandra sucked in a breath. She glared at Maggie and then turned to Patrick. "Your loss! You're nothing! I heard how you screwed up tryouts. I'm sure you'll screw up training camp too. So you can just go to hell."

She stomped away and suddenly veered to the side as one of her heels broke in the hard rutted road. She yanked both heels off, turned, and threw them at Patrick's head.

He ducked just in time. Then she stomped off—barefoot and bitchy.

Patrick turned to Maggie. "Now can we talk?"

"Yeah," she said. "Over here." She led him a short walk away to the closed liquor store next door.

They settled side by side on the front step, silent for a moment. Maggie still had a bad feeling in her gut. Finally she broke the silence. "Is this the part where you tell me it's been fun, but we can't see each other anymore?"

"I don't want to hurt you," Patrick said. Which meant he planned on doing exactly that. She could read between the lines. She sighed. He had warned her right from the beginning that he didn't want to hurt her. Maybe she should've taken that as a big sign that he would.

"Just say it," she said.

"I need to focus one hundred percent on football."

"So football players can't have girlfriends?" She knew that wasn't true. The proof had just walked away spitting mad moments ago.

"No, *I* can't have a girlfriend. It's not you. I'm not going to be with anybody."

Her gut twisted painfully. He'd said he loved her. Why would that change just because he got a call to go to training camp? She glanced over at him staring straight ahead, elbows on his knees, and suddenly she knew. He'd only wanted her when he couldn't have football. She was a consolation prize. And now that he had what he really wanted, he was dumping her. She thought for once she came first for someone.

"Why're you doing this?" she asked. She wanted to hear him say it. To admit that she was a placeholder until something better came along. Second best.

"It's nothing personal," Patrick said quietly.

She stood and glared down at him. "At least you can be honest with me! Don't I deserve that much?"

"I am being honest. I need to give one hundred percent to football. You knew that's who I was."

"I thought you were more than that."

He didn't reply.

"I deserve better than this," she told him, drawing on the last shred of pride she had before she completely broke down.

"You do," he said easily. "You deserve the best, Maggie. I'm sorry."

She bit back the scream of frustration she wanted to let out. "Bye."

"Bye."

He didn't move, so she did. One foot in front of the other, stiff and silent, a walking corpse, dead inside. Because Patrick was holding her crushed and bloody heart in his hands.

~

Patrick thought for sure he'd done the right thing ending things with Maggie, but here it was Monday morning, he was about to leave Fieldridge and Maggie for good, and he felt like shit. His uncle wasn't sympathetic. Quinn had spilled all the gory details of what had happened at the diner to his uncle, and Uncle Todd was definitely on Maggie's side. So much so that he'd tortured Patrick for a good hour this morn-ing, showing him the stunning flyers and pictures that Maggie had taken. Seeing his carnie family in action got him choked up. Somehow she'd captured how they really were, beyond their sometimes odd appearances and quirky person-alities. They looked fun, loving, like they were putting on the best show on earth for whoever hired them. It was amazing, a work of art, really.

"Well, Patricky," Uncle Todd said, "we're pulling out in an hour. Last chance to bring her along."

Patrick gritted his teeth. They'd talked about this. There was no point in bringing Maggie along for the next six weeks of carnival because they'd have to say goodbye all over again when he went to training camp. It was easier to end things now. Though he had to admit the past four days had been hell. He'd catch glimpses of her as she took pictures around town and during the carnival. Every time she caught him looking, she'd turn away, chin in the air. She was pissed. Rightfully so. That was good. It would make it easier for her to move on. He'd rather have her mad than sobbing over him.

"She's mad at me," Patrick said. "Even if I asked her, she'd probably spit in my eye."

Uncle Todd slapped Patrick on the shoulder. "She might be mad, but that doesn't mean she hates you."

Patrick's shoulders slumped. "She should."

"Shoulda, coulda, woulda," Uncle Todd said in a singsong voice. "I told you she wasn't like Scarlett." Again with the *Gone with the Wind* reference to his ex.

"Sandra," Patrick said through his teeth.

"Maggie doesn't hold a grudge." His uncle held up a

picture. "This is how she sees you, and I don't see a football in that picture, do you?"

The picture was Patrick wearing a rainbow clown wig, cheeks blown out as he made a balloon animal for a five-year-old girl with pigtails while younger kids looked on in wonder. His uncle flipped the picture over. On the back Maggie had written, *My favorite picture of him. Thought you might like to have it.*

He stared at it. Why would this be Maggie's favorite picture of him? She didn't even like clowns. Of course, he wasn't wearing clown makeup. He wore his regular clothes, but he'd added the wig at the last minute when he took over for his uncle on break. He turned to his uncle. "I don't get it. She doesn't like clowns."

His uncle socked his shoulder. Hard. "She sees how you really are! On the inside where it fucking counts. Your heart, Patrick!"

The truth hit him like a hard tackle—Maggie loved him with or without football. And he had to do the same. He had heart. That was what made him a good football player, and that was what made him fall hard for Maggie. It wasn't about one hundred percent focus on football. To be the best he could be, he had to juggle career and the people he loved. He needed both to keep his heart full. It was a risk. But Maggie was worth it.

"She's at town hall to find out about business licensing," his uncle said.

Patrick leapt to his feet, headed to the door, and stopped, hand on the knob. "Thanks," he said over his shoulder. "I owe you one."

"Meh. It was nothing. Just make sure you name your first-born after me." Uncle Todd winked.

Patrick barked out a laugh and raced out the door and down the block to town hall. He took the steps two at a time and burst inside, looking around wildly for where she could be. He found a small directory labeling the few rooms, strode down the hall and burst in.

"Patrick!" Maggie exclaimed. She wore the same outfit as

the first day they'd met this summer. A white blouse cut low enough in front to show some cleavage, pink short pants, and flip-flops. So sexy. His beautiful magical goddess. He pulled her right out of her seat and hugged her.

"Excuse me," an authoritative female voice said from behind the other side of the desk. "We're in the middle of a meeting."

"I'm sorry," Patrick said to the other woman. "But this is important. I need to give her a big apology and beg her to come back to me."

Maggie's eyes widened. "Can I have a minute, Alice?"

"Is it true love?" Alice asked in a haughty voice, but a hint of a smile played over her lips. "Because that's the only interruption I'll accept."

Maggie turned to Patrick, a question in her eyes. He never wanted her to have another minute's doubt about that. "Yes, it is," he said, never taking his eyes off Maggie.

Alice patted Patrick's shoulder. "Go for it. You have fifteen minutes." She sailed out the door.

Patrick turned to Maggie. "I love you."

She blinked.

He barreled on, needing to get it all out. "I'm an idiot. I never should've let you go. I'm sorry. So very sorry. And I might have nothing to my name, or I might have a lot to my name, and if you're okay with that, I'd love for you to come with me. You can do your photography stuff. And we've got to get you to some auditions. Your dreams matter too. And I love you and want to be with you. I know I said I need to be one hundred percent football, but what I really need is to be one hundred percent you." He felt like he'd just run up and down the bleachers a hundred times. Breathless and buzzed with adrenaline.

She slapped a hand over her mouth, blinking rapidly.

He sucked in air. Was it too late?

"Maggie, please say something."

~

The lump in Maggie's throat made it difficult to speak. Patrick was making her his priority over football, his dream career? He was putting her first? No one had ever put her first.

Patrick shoved a hand in his hair. "Tell me to get lost, or tell me—"

"I'm your first choice?" she asked in a small voice.

He grabbed her hands and squeezed gently. "You'll always be first in my heart."

Her lower lip trembled. She didn't want to cry. This was a good thing. It was just so overwhelming to be first in someone's heart. She threw herself in his arms.

His arms wrapped tightly around her, and he kissed her hair. "I thought I'd lost you," he said. "I'm so glad you don't hold a grudge."

She squeezed him around the middle and then wiped her eyes. "Does this mean I get to be a carnie for a while? Your uncle invited me before."

He pushed a lock of hair behind her ear. "Thank God for Uncle Todd. He said we can have our own trailer. The jazz polka cowboy left for a jazz polka band."

"He did? Wow. And then you'll go to training camp?"

"Yes, in August."

"And then…" She waited for him to fill in the sentence with something gloriously romantic.

He stroked her cheek. "If I get a contract, you can travel with me. You could take pictures the whole way. I'll have more than enough money for both of us." That did sound romantic, but—

"And if you don't get a contract?"

"Then we'll come up with a plan B together."

She melted. She really liked the sound of that.

He kissed her tenderly. "I love you so much. I'm sorry I fumbled this. From here on out, we're a team."

She beamed. It still felt like a miracle to her that they'd found each other. Two such very different people who fit perfectly together.

"I love you so much too!" she exclaimed before wrapping

her arms around his neck and kissing him with all the love in her heart. He deepened the kiss, and she lost herself. There was nothing but heat and passion and true love. Happiness bubbled up inside her, filling her with exuberant energy.

She broke the kiss. "Hold that thought."

She pulled away to an open area across the room and did her happy dance, a chorus of stamping feet and then arms in the air, leaping for joy. Once, twice, three times. He laughed.

"I had to!" she exclaimed. "You made one of my dreams come true!"

He cocked his head. "Which one was that?"

"Being a carnie. I fell in love with everyone here."

"Don't forget the second dream. Me."

She ran and leaped into his arms, wrapping her arms and legs around him tightly. Then she grabbed his head and peppered him with kisses. "Yes, you, Patrick. Always you."

"You're my dream. Always you."

His lips met hers and things heated quickly. He turned and pressed her against the wall, his hard planes against her softness, making her throb with need. She moaned as he pressed against her through her thin pants.

Someone knocked on the door and then it swung open. "You'll have to take your true love to a more private location," Alice announced.

Patrick grabbed her hand and they ran out the door, laughing, ready for the next part of their lives. Together.

EPILOGUE

Fifteen years later...

Patrick was back at home with his family in Clover Park, Connecticut, and happy to be there. He and Maggie had married right before training camp began, which meant a lot to him because he knew she loved him whether or not he ultimately earned a football contract. As it turned out, he had. He was newly retired from the New York Titans, the team that had given him his start and gave him a great career—three-time league MVP, two-time Super Bowl champ, and fifteen-time leader in catches, receiving yards, and touchdowns. He was proud of his performance, but he was even more proud of Maggie, who not only excelled at every creative thing she tried, but also had the acting career she'd hoped for. Her big break was on a crazy sci-fi show that suited her perfectly as a time-traveling detective. Plus she'd done a lot of commercials and modeling work. Who could resist her bubbly exuberance?

"Hey, Crazy Feet, catch!" Maggie hollered before taking off at a run barefoot through the grass of their backyard, heading straight for him. The nickname was because during his first pro game, he scored a touchdown and did Maggie's happy dance to let her know he was thinking of her. The fans loved it and dubbed him Crazy Feet.

She leaped and he caught her, kissing her long and deep, as in love with her now as he was the very first day they met.

"Gross!" their fourteen-year-old son, Jack, said. "Bad enough you have a picture of kissing in your room. Do you have to do it in real life too?"

Maggie had framed the picture she took of them kissing on top of the Ferris wheel during their first carnival together. She hung it above their bed every place they'd lived since then from trailer to hotel to house.

They hadn't forgotten to add in Uncle Todd's name with their firstborn. He was Jack Todd O'Hare. It was, after all, Uncle Todd who'd made it possible for him and Maggie to be together that first summer. Uncle Todd was still going strong, and they loved visiting the carnival every summer with a lot of the same people Patrick and Maggie knew and loved.

The Fellini brothers had passed away five years ago, within days of each other, all of them in their late nineties. After the first brother passed, the others told his uncle where to find a surprising amount of cash they'd stashed away in tin cans. They asked him to use it to make someone's dream come true. And, after Uncle Todd talked to every member of the carnie family, he decided that special someone would be Quinn the corn dog man. Uncle Todd paid for a private acting coach. Now Quinn starred in movies, mostly as the villain, though he wanted to branch out to a heroic role. His stutter was gone for good.

Maggie laughed, her blue eyes sparkling with mischief and fun. "Put me down. I think the kissing monster's coming for Jack!" Patrick set her down and she took off after their son. She wouldn't be able to catch him unless he wanted to be caught. Ever since Jack's growth spurt, he'd gained some serious speed. He played quarterback on the local team, and he had a powerful passing arm. The other players called him Lightning.

Maggie caught Jack around the waist and kissed him all

over his cheek. Jack wiggled out of her arms. "Mo-o-om, gross!" He wiped his cheek, but he looked happy.

Maggie ruffled Jack's hair. "One day you'll want to kiss a girl."

Jack turned red.

Patrick and Maggie exchanged an amused look.

His heart squeezed. He was so damn lucky.

"Will you practice passing with me, Dad?" Jack asked.

"Sure, get the ball."

Jack took off for the shed where they kept all the sports equipment.

Maggie called their son her greatest gift. She called him Crazy Feet or Patrick or sometimes her personal sex god. Naturally.

And Patrick called her by the name she embodied in every way—goddess.

Be sure to check out my spinoff Happy Endings Book Club series, also set in Clover Park, featuring the irresistibly sexy Campbell brothers (and a tomboy sister) who find love with the help of the matchmaking leader of the Happy Endings Book Club. Get started with book 1, *Hidden Hollywood*. Join the club and get your happy ending!

Hidden Hollywood
She's on top…
When superstar actress Claire Jordan researched her role for the Fierce Trilogy movies, she never expected the bond she feels with the author and her romance book club aka the Happy Endings Book Club. Soon Claire finds herself confessing her secret longing for a regular guy—no more egocentric wealthy players—and the book club is all too ready to help. In disguise as a regular girl, she's all set for a date with book-club-approved Josh Campbell.

He's on top…
Billionaire tech CEO Jake Campbell is weary of gold-digging women, especially the glamorous superficial types. So when his identical twin, Josh, calls in a favor, asking Jake to step in as him on a date, Jake figures one of Josh's cute girl-next-door types might be just what he needs. One night of passion with the sweet girl next door leaves Jake wanting more, except she seems to have vanished.

Sometimes a Happy Ending is just the beginning.

Sign up for my newsletter and never miss a new release! https://www.kyliegilmore.com/newsletter

ALSO BY KYLIE GILMORE

Unleashed Romance <<steamy romcoms with dogs!

Fetching (Book 1)

Dashing (Book 2)

Sporting (Book 3)

Toying (Book 4)

Blazing (Book 5)

Chasing (Book 6)

Daring (Book 7)

Leading (Book 8)

Racing (Book 9)

Loving (Book 10)

The Clover Park Series <<brothers who put family first!

The Opposite of Wild (Book 1)

Daisy Does It All (Book 2)

Bad Taste in Men (Book 3)

Kissing Santa (Book 4)

Restless Harmony (Book 5)

Not My Romeo (Book 6)

Rev Me Up (Book 7)

An Ambitious Engagement (Book 8)

Clutch Player (Book 9)

A Tempting Friendship (Book 10)

Clover Park Bride: Nico and Lily's Wedding

A Valentine's Day Gift (Book 11)

Maggie Meets Her Match (Book 12)

The Clover Park Charmers series <<sweet and sexy charmers!

Almost Over It (Book 1)

Almost Married (Book 2)

Almost Fate (Book 3)

Almost in Love (Book 4)

Almost Romance (Book 5)

Almost Hitched (Book 6)

Happy Endings Book Club Series <<the Campbell family and a romance book club collide!

Hidden Hollywood (Book 1)

Inviting Trouble (Book 2)

So Revealing (Book 3)

Formal Arrangement (Book 4)

Bad Boy Done Wrong (Book 5)

Mess With Me (Book 6)

Resisting Fate (Book 7)

Chance of Romance (Book 8)

Wicked Flirt (Book 9)

An Inconvenient Plan (Book 10)

A Happy Endings Wedding (Book 11)

The Rourkes Series <<swoonworthy princes and kickass princesses!

Royal Catch (Book 1)

Royal Hottie (Book 2)

Royal Darling (Book 3)

Royal Charmer (Book 4)

Royal Player (Book 5)

Royal Shark (Book 6)

Rogue Prince (Book 7)

Rogue Gentleman (Book 8)

Rogue Rascal (Book 9)

Rogue Angel (Book 10)

Rogue Devil (Book 11)

Rogue Beast (Book 12)

**Check out my website for the most up-to-date list of my books:
kyliegilmore.com/books**

ABOUT THE AUTHOR

Kylie Gilmore is the *USA Today* bestselling author of over fifty humorous contemporary romances. Her series include Unleashed Romance, the Rourkes, the Happy Endings Book Club, Clover Park, and Clover Park Charmers. With more than three million downloads of her books, readers all over the world love escaping into her hilarious feel-good romances featuring strong bonds with family, friends, and community.

Kylie lives in New York with her family, a demanding cat, and a nutso dog. When she's not writing, reading hot romance, or dutifully taking notes at writing conferences, you can find her flexing her muscles all the way to the high cabinet for her secret chocolate stash.

Sign up for Kylie's Newsletter and get a FREE book! kyliegilmore.com/newsletter

For text alerts on Kylie's new releases, text KYLIE to the number (888) 707-3025. (US only)

For more fun stuff check out Kylie's website https://www.kyliegilmore.com.

Thanks for reading *Maggie Meets Her Match*. I hope you enjoyed it. Would you like to know about new releases? You can sign up for my new release email list at https://www.kyliegilmore.com/newsletter. I promise not to clog your inbox! Only new release info, sales, and some fun giveaways.

I love to hear from readers! You can find me at:
kyliegilmore.com
Instagram.com/kyliegilmore
Facebook.com/KylieGilmoreToo
Twitter @KylieGilmoreToo

If you liked Patrick and Maggie's story, please leave a review on your favorite retailer's website or Goodreads. Thank you.